PRETERNATURAL

BOOK 3

RECKONING

God Help Us...

PETER TOPSIDE

Preternatural Reckoning

Copyright © 2022 Peter Topside

Published by Meadowsville Quill, LLC

Paperback ISBN: 978-1-7363472-2-5

eISBN: 978-1-7363472-3-2

Cover and Interior Design: GKS Creative

Project Management: The Cadence Group

Editing: Monti Shalosky and Kimberly A. Bookless

I want to thank my literary colleagues and enthusiasts, friends, family, and everyone from Smith Publicity and The Cadence Group. When I had lost all hope and never thought I would accomplish a lifelong goal of publishing the first Preternatural story, you gave me the means to persevere. And not only did I publish book one, despite all the troubled production with it, I then was able to create two sequels. I am so thrilled and humbled to be able to share the exciting conclusion of this trilogy with the world. I hope you all have as much fun reading these stories as I did writing them. None of it would have happened without all your resources, love, and support.

Thank you all!

Contents

Current Events

A fresh morning saw Meadowsville's Lucerne Lake as a beautiful sight. The town was shrouded by the surrounding foliage, and bits of the dawn's early light trickling in kept shadows on the water's imperfections. The buildup on the surface, the caution signs, and all visuals of abnormalities were still hidden. As the sun rose, there were no more secrets, and all was revealed. Much like Meadowsville, the true ugliness was exposed in the present times, and the severity of the issues in this body of water, and in the town at large, had yet to fully culminate.

It'd been a full year since Blackheart was put to rest by Alexandra Hughes. Her evolution to a powerful leader was complete, and she felt competent not only to lead her church but also to manage any issues that could arise. Any previous doubts of her knowledge, skills, and abilities were put to rest, along with Blackheart, one year ago. The town now looked up to her as their savior, as she demonstrated that only she knew how to put the monster down once and for all. Beyond the brute force that Christian Reed had displayed, she had outsmarted the beast and bested him in every way.

She remained the head of the Meadowsville Community Church, and due to her increased popularity, many community members had left other local houses of worship to join her there. As good as her intentions might have been, many of her fellow church leaders had become envious, going as far as to ignore any communications from her, shun their former members, and publicly denounce the Meadowsville Community Church's efforts to improve the town. These same leaders had fallen into the old habits of the town at large, being more consumed with the monetary aspects of their houses of worship than the spiritual well-being of the inhabitants. Many of them commiserated together in private, trying to figure out a way to possibly work with Alexandra, as they also wanted to keep the town afloat and knew how important they all were in those efforts. However, as they were forced to lay off their office staff, reduce celebratory events, and even go into debt just to keep the lights on in their sites, all stemming from the reduced income from their congregations, each one of them became soured on the very idea of working with Alexandra.

Alexandra had taken notice of all these happenings; she did her best to remedy the issue but had not made much headway. Very few of the other religious leaders would even say hello to her, let alone discuss the problem at hand. And while she wanted to continue the efforts to mend any hurt feelings from recent events, she tried to maintain her focus on the bigger picture. Her main priority was that Meadowsville needed to continue progressing toward salvation and not revert to its old ways, which had brought nothing but increasingly terrible misfortune to them previously. The cycle needed to be permanently disrupted.

Remembering how everyone had laughed at Christian Reed for predicting the creature's return, Alexandra did not want to take even the slightest chance of it happening again. They all needed to band together and denounce the strength and presence of Blackheart, which would be the only and ultimate way to keep him from returning. And, as much as she would prefer to have an alliance with the other church leaders, it was not a necessity. She felt that if they continued to put their own vanity ahead of the welfare of the town, she would rather work alone and keep the integrity of her efforts intact. And she was now confident enough to do it all on her own.

Christian was still recovering from his various injuries, now suffering from varying levels of chronic pain. He was no longer able to stand up from a chair without feeling as if his knees were on fire, and he couldn't even take the garbage out to the curb without struggling to keep his balance. He had good and bad days but tried to stay physically active to combat the effects of his painful arthritis and discomfort. Blackheart did a great deal of damage to him during their last encounter, but Christian survived and was now grateful for another chance at life. He would never let himself jeopardize his own health or his family's safety again.

After his heroics last year, Mayor Wiggins put him in charge of a specialized division of the police department, the Meadowsville Paranormal Squad—MPS for short—that was aimed solely at dealing with potentially supernatural occurrences. What was once a gigantic secret was now fully acknowledged and appreciated by both residents and township administration alike. On the rare occasions that someone cast doubt on Blackheart's supernatural abilities, there was always a fellow resident nearby to provide picture proof of the most recent events—for example, the cell phone tower that was uprooted by the beast. There was no debating what happened one year ago, not even by the most prudent doubters.

Once Christian was sworn into the police department, Wiggins quickly put together the MPS. The department mandate now stated that all new officers had to spend a year in this division before moving to regular duty, to be aware of the town's strange history and how to be prepared and properly manage such unique situations. And Christian, of course, was the best person to guide such a group, as he had encountered Blackheart more times than anyone else. He mainly stayed in the police station, due to his limited mobility, but did go out with the team every so often to keep his skills intact. He enjoyed his new calling and felt he was truly making a difference.

On the home front, Rebecca, Adam, and Christian were also closer than ever. Christian began receiving mental health treatment and had been working hard on regulating himself.

His new therapist taught him strategies to manage his emotions and triggers rather than allowing his anger and old habits to dominate every decision. And his prior medication regimen was completely changed by his psychiatrist, which kept him at ease. While he found it very difficult to stick with his new treatments, he knew if he didn't fight his inner demons with everything he had, he would end up losing his family. Losing his daughter, Caroline, was hard enough to stomach, but having the same happen to others would be too much for him to handle. And he would not allow that.

Rebecca was thankful each and every day that her husband was almost back to the man she fell in love with all those years ago. She spent many years praying and hoping he would find peace with himself, and, despite the various obstacles and circumstances, he was almost there. He was no longer patrolling Chrysanthemum Drive or keeping her up at night as she wondered whether he would be arrested or killed for overreacting to something in town. That was all now a distant memory. When she would walk past Caroline's bedroom, becoming choked up sometimes, looking at the relic, he was there for her. After all that time having to smother her feelings, afraid to speak to Christian due to his instability, she had her partner again. And for the first time, Adam also now had a father in his life. Growing up after the initial conflict between his father and Blackheart, Adam didn't know him well. Christian had either been patrolling the town, cleaning his battle gear, or tuning his weapons, and there had been very little importance placed on his relationship with his son.

Adam, while still getting used to the idea of having an active set of parents now, was tolerating the change rather well. He now placed his father on a symbolic pedestal, admiring his willingness to make the ultimate sacrifice to save their town. Christian had shared some of the research he had done on John Smith and Blackheart over the past years, and Adam was fascinated. He had never enjoyed any of his history classes in school but now wanted to know more about Meadowsville.

As the town also worked to repair itself from Blackheart's last attack, the budget was in shambles, worse than ever. Mayor Wiggins was doing his best to avoid layoffs of his municipal workers but would have no choice if things didn't improve quickly. Absent a miracle, there was no sign of any such thing. One councilman had proposed creating a memorial for all citizens who died at the hands of Mr. Smith and Blackheart over the years on Chrysanthemum Drive. He also floated the concept of possibly rebuilding the mansion and remediating the land to his fellow council members and was slowly gaining support. The strange occurrences at the hands of their favorite malevolent beings were still popular outside their town, but with nothing to present to potential tourists anymore, there was no reason for anyone to visit.

While Wiggins was growing up, he hated seeing the town in its prior "glory" during the height of its issues, but it was nice to see so many people from all over the country coming in to visit—even if for the wrong reasons. Although the neighboring cities and towns had isolated Meadowsville, it didn't matter because people were flooding in to see the legend of John Smith.

Wiggins wanted to create new outreaches to show the towns around them that Meadowsville had changed. Some showing of goodwill would bring in people from outside the town and end the longstanding opinion that Meadowsville was cursed, media-hungry, and desperate.

Given the town's terrible reputation, which had been formed in the early days, anyone immediately outside of the Meadowsville city limits ignored the town. The supposed tall tales of monsters were always laughed off as financially beneficial ploys. Any reports of missing persons were also deemed fake, and eyewitness accounts weren't even acknowledged. But with the best intentions, Mayor Wiggins needed to work on creating something important and meaningful in his town. He had recently offered to allow the other police departments to come see how the MPS functioned, as they might want to consider something similar for their towns. It wasn't likely, but it was another act of good faith.

The biggest obstacle continued to be the fire and police department restorations, which were an immediate priority after their destruction last year by Blackheart. Lucerne Lake was also having major issues, but unfortunately, it would have to wait. Because of the previous issues in the town, property insurance companies refused to cover any of the repairs unless the premiums skyrocketed to an unimaginable rate. With Mayor Wiggins being forced to cover the repairs from what was left in the dwindling budget, any last bit of surplus was gone. Most of his ideas were pushed to the bottom of the priority list, which stunted any efforts. Despite the barriers he faced, Wiggins had no choice but to plunge the town into a very bad financial situation, with the hope of bringing about greater profits and eventually being able to dig out of the debt. He wondered whether Blackheart had created his very specific path of destruction last year knowing it would trigger a series of events that would bring another dark period onto Meadowsville. He never dared say it out loud to anyone else, but such a thought kept him up at night, unsure how to prepare his town.

2

Family Time

Christian hugged Alexandra as she walked into the Reeds' house for their normal Wednesday night dinner. She made sure to take off her shoes and put them on the mat to her left, being respectful of the Reeds' home. Adam and Rebecca both came out of the kitchen to show her the same affection, giving her a nice warm welcome, which was much appreciated by Alexandra. She smelled the air, and her olfactory sense was delighted at the aroma coming from the stovetop.

Rebecca went back into the kitchen to finish making sloppy joe sandwiches. Adam did the dishes, scrubbing the cutting boards of all the loose pieces of onion and green pepper, and then set the table as Christian sat with Alex. He placed the forks cockeyed to tease at his father's obsessive-compulsive habits. It wasn't to be mean but just to be playful with Christian.

Christian and Alexandra smiled at one another, alone in the living room. Christian muted the local TV news to give her his full attention. Compared to where their relationship was a year ago, as well as both of their lives, they were two completely different people now. Alexandra looked around at their family pictures, seeing one from when Caroline was still alive and Christian and Rebecca were much younger. She smiled, knowing how much they still missed their daughter and conflicted by David's heinous action the night she was killed. Alexandra wanted to defend him, knowing the intense struggles with his vampire abilities, but what he had done was inexcusable.

The Reeds' house also never changed, which she questioned but assumed was an attempt to try to hold on to their loss, as neither Christian nor Rebecca were ready to move on from it. Alexandra chose to keep her thoughts to herself to avoid offending anyone in the Reed family.

"Can you believe it's been a year?" Christian asked, lounging in his recliner.

"Yes, 'cause I still think about it every day. Not one of those things that you forget so easily," she replied, sitting on the couch.

"Whatta ya think of them rebuilding his house?" Christian referred to Blackheart.

"Is that a definite? I thought it was just chatter at a council meeting?" Alexandra asked, becoming more alert, remembering Blackheart's feral and terrifying face.

"Well, the idea is to rebuild it as a tourist attraction and also make a nice memorial for the victims too. A few of the council members are on board with it now. I spoke with Wiggins yesterday; he's trying to figure any other way out, but what was originally a last resort now appears to be very viable. He told me how sorry he was that he even brought it up to them, but there's no going back from it now. Even if he resists it, it's very likely that he'll be overruled if they all choose to move forward with it."

"I don't know what to think about it. I'm more scared than anything at what's in that land. So, while I want to say it'll be okay, I can't. They have to be really careful. I—" she began, hoping Christian would understand where her thoughts were headed.

"The answer is yes. They're going to remediate the land before building. No more blood in the soil and no issues," he said calmly, cutting her off.

"But Smith is buried somewhere on the property."

"That's the story, but who knows for sure? No one has ever looked into it further."

"I wish we knew more of how this works. Blackheart was kept alive down there for fifteen years, even after being killed by you and David. Smith supposedly died of natural causes, so his body is probably still fully intact. So could he come back somehow? Or is he gone for good?" she asked, concerned.

"I dunno. Let's hope not. I can't handle another round with those things. I couldn't really handle the first few," Christian said jokingly, acting like it hurt him to laugh.

Alexandra sat in silence for a few seconds before politely smiling at Christian, feeling terror in her soul at the thought of Blackheart and Smith returning. She now felt a sense of urgency to reach out again to her colleagues. She had a bad feeling about where things were headed in Meadowsville.

Rebecca began plating dinner for everyone as the scent of the hearty meal filled the room. The clanking of the plates disrupted Alexandra's thoughts, which was not necessarily a bad thing. Rebecca cut the large, puffy kaiser rolls in half and plopped a big serving of the meat mixture on top of each bottom piece.

Christian saw the despair in his friend's eyes but didn't know what to say. He was working with Mayor Wiggins to take all precautions, if this project was to proceed.

Alexandra changed the subject. "So how's the new job?"

"It's really good. Feel like I'm finally doing something good to help this place. And Wiggins was telling me that other towns are looking at this as a pilot program. They all have their own problems, much like we did, so hopefully it helps them too. This is my first set of recruits, so I'm doing my best to keep everything together."

"That's good."

"How are you?"

"Fine," she responded unconvincingly.

"How are you?" he persisted, prodding for a sincerer response, giving her a stern yet soft look.

"Better. Like, the church still has the highest membership numbers ever, but it leveled off a bit, and I've noticed a small decline each week. But the other churches aren't real thrilled with that. It was never my intention to take from anyone," she said, exasperated.

"I can imagine. That's a hard situation. Have any of the others reached out?"

"No. I've tried so many times but got nothing back. I've even gone there, but they still won't even have a conversation with me. I have to keep trying though."

"They'll come around. Have to at some point."

"Let's hope so. I think keeping our faith strong, especially from what we've all been through here, is not something that should be taken lightly. Especially not for money or reputation. If we all start to fall back into old habits and not working with each other, it leaves us vulnerable. And who knows what type of evil can be brought here again."

"Agreed," he said, sipping some water, having serious thoughts on the concerns Alexandra raised.

"Dinner's up," Rebecca called as Adam brought everything to the table.

Christian leaned on the armrests and slowly stood up with a great effort. Alex tried to help him, but he politely waved her off to do it himself. Today was not the best day to be his feet, as his knees roared with pain. He stood up straight and looked at the television, to see the final repairs at the police department had been completed.

They all sat down to enjoy the delicious meal after Alexandra said a very brief prayer of thanks. "Bless this meal, the company we have here at this table, and for all the wonderful things you do for us each and every day. We love and appreciate you, Lord."

As she finished the prayer, she kept quiet for another few seconds and said some more to God in her mind. *God, I am so scared at what may be on the horizon. Please keep me strong and capable to continue leading this town to its salvation. I need you. We need you more than ever.*

The Reeds responded with "Amen" as Alexandra looked up, taking a few deep breaths. She was the first to take a bite of her sandwich, with its perfect texture and rich flavor. She was not one to like spice in her food, but this had just enough to tickle the back of her tongue, and it worked so well for the dish.

"So, Adam, how's everything at school?" she asked.

"It's okay. It's school. I'm going to be assigned a big research project soon, so we'll see where that goes." He watched Christian as he spoke.

"You'll ace it," Rebecca said to him, smiling.

Christian smiled, and Alex watched how Adam just admired his father now. The dynamic between them was healthy and satisfying to behold, especially after such a rocky few months last year.

"Any idea what it's about yet?" Christian inquired.

"Not yet. I'm hoping I can do something about Blackheart or Mr. Smith."

Everyone stopped eating briefly, thinking of their own feelings at that notion.

"Well, what would you want to do with that?" Alex asked, trying to break up the tense moment.

"See if I can piece together how the town started, the founding families, and then the progression into both of the creatures. There has to be some concrete links among it all. And no one has seemed to figure it out yet. Or at least they haven't made it public. Whatever the case is. But that's my goal. I think it could be really fun to do."

"Shit, I'd read it," Christian said.

Alex gave him a quick, playful eyebrow raise at the curse. Christian made it a point not to look at her but felt her condemning gaze. "If I don't see you, it's not a sin," he said teasingly.

Christian bit into his sandwich and a chunk of the meat mixture slopped down onto his plate, splattering tomato sauce onto his previously untarnished white T-shirt. He paused, not sure of whether to clean up or keep eating, but ended up continuing his meal.

"Honey, tell the teacher your idea. I'm sure he'll go for it," Rebecca said, ignoring Christian's antics.

Adam smiled and realized he had dropped food on himself too. He and Christian smirked at each other while Alex and Rebecca rolled their eyes. They continued with the meal and enjoyed each other's company for the next few hours. Alexandra discussed the upcoming *Peter Pan* play that Rebecca's elementary school would be hosting in a few short months. She had flyers in the church vestibule and had seen them all over the town too.

3

Cast Down

Blackheart stood in an empty field with picture-perfect trees all around the perimeter and a bright, beautiful blue sky with no clouds overhead. A warm, gentle wind touched his now flawless face. He had no more scars, disfigurements, or anything different than a normal person. But his body had a slight glow to it, and his movements were slower and more fluid. His bare feet felt the gentle blades of grass as they swayed. He had been in this same environment for an entire year, but somehow it didn't get tiresome, despite seeming like a purgatory. He always pictured heaven as a more profound and amazing place with all sorts of wondrous people and sights, but this was not what he imagined. It was sort of a letdown.

He still felt the burden of his parents being killed, the years of torture with Smith, and all the things that contributed to his wicked ways. All the afterlife did was relieve his worries; it didn't resolve anything from his time on earth. It was if God continued to give him mediocrity and tried to sway him into thinking it was what he needed and wanted. *Mind games, just like with John Smith.* Blackheart still nursed a sense of entitlement and felt he deserved better.

He had also begun to wonder how him demanding the same of Meadowsville compared to God's expectation on mankind. And he came up empty-handed each time the thought crossed his mind. So why was he not comparable to Him? What was so different in how they operated? Blackheart was sure God heard these thoughts and felt his feelings, but he couldn't suppress them. He had a right to know why he couldn't be at God's level of power. Just like on earth, he never fully understood Him and wasn't able to figure out how to properly bring himself before God. However, once he saw the undeniable potential in Alexandra, he knew she would be the one to bring about his final earthly demise. From the first time he encountered her and told her she was as close to God as Blackheart could get, he knew she was special. He sensed it from her. She was different than the others he encountered. Not like any other man or woman he'd victimized over his life. She was unbreakable and unattainable. And while he placed a great deal of responsibility on her shoulders, she did not disappoint. She guided him to death, beyond his own understanding at the time, and brought him before God, which was exactly what he wanted to do all along.

He was no longer afraid of God and now saw what the heavens looked like and God's power and love. *But it wasn't enough for me.* He did not see his dead parents or anyone else from his past that he cared for. It was just him and the spirit of God at all times. While peaceful on an epic level, he could withstand it no longer. He began to view God no differently than John Smith, who kept him locked in that cellar for so many years, imposing a lifestyle on him that he never asked for.

And I overcame my abuser and became something much more than Smith could have ever anticipated. This situation with him and God held a strong similarity, and that was unacceptable.

"What makes you better than me?" he thought, directing it at God, pushing Him to respond. "Why are you so entitled and able to rule over everything in the universe, expecting everyone to follow your bidding?"

As he had such a thought again, the trees surrounding the field were sucked into the ground and the wind stopped. There was no noise, only silence. The air thickened and Blackheart felt tension build. The blue sky transitioned into a light red. God was not seen but felt. Blackheart understood what he had done—he had too many impure thoughts against his creator. Despite some apprehension, he did not cower. He stood tall, feeling meek and fearful, observing the power of God, who expressed His displeasure. He began to feel God speak to him telepathically, asking him why he was in heaven.

"To witness You. Your glory. To find—" he responded telepathically but stopped without a proper ending to his sentence.

God paused as the sky turned deep red, reflecting his feelings. He asked Blackheart why he could not accept his love and be at peace.

"I don't think I can ever find peace."

God relayed that Blackheart was at peace yet his soul yearned for more, which He could not provide.

"I need more. I want more. Your love is not enough."

God asked why Blackheart believed he deserved more.

"Because what I've seen of your power in the last year has made me want what you have more than ever. You command an entire universe. Any world. Any species. It's all yours. And you fear someone like me who could eventually rise up to your level. Give people something else to believe in so they forget you. You are afraid of anyone else becoming like you, because you'd be an afterthought. Not at the forefront, the way you like to be. Faith and love is what gives you your strength."

God said Blackheart could not have that kind of power and wasn't ready to be there yet. Blackheart felt God's sadness as their interaction continued. He felt bad for hurting God but understood that he needed to be true to himself above all else. He truly felt he had unfinished work to do and could not be at eternal peace until he reached his full potential.

"I want this. All of it. And I'll do whatever I need to," Blackheart said, now feeling much like himself on earth, only with greater power and abilities now.

The sky suddenly went black, and the grass disappeared. There was just darkness.

Blackheart levitated upward, trying to find a beginning or end to this nothingness, but there was nothing there. He began to remember his time reigning over Meadowsville and how he felt like a god. The feeling of having complete control was intoxicating and satisfying. He imagined how it would feel to reign over not just a single town but the entire world. To take God's supposed greatest creation away from him and make it his own. If Meadowsville's faith gave him as much power as God had, expanding to greater territories and getting billions and billions to worship him, it would possibly enable to him to be powerful enough to challenge God formally. He became dizzy at the thought of so much power. No one and nothing could stop him.

The immediate and strong connection to God severed, and Blackheart abruptly fell for what seemed like an eternity. His heavenly form began to be manipulated yet his enhanced abilities remained intact somehow. With the sheer force of his fiery plummet, he was unable to utilize any of them.

He reached terminal velocity, and his skin burned from the fire around his body as the earth came clearly into view. God underestimated Blackheart to just send him back to earth again. They had a standoff now, and Blackheart refused to yield to Him.

As Blackheart got closer and closer, the seas disappeared into the distance, the continents began to expand below, the clouds parted, and Meadowsville came into view from miles above. He grinned and readied himself for impact. He crashed into the ground with a thunderous sound, shaking almost the entire state. His body smoldered as the flames extinguished, and he got up and moved around, totally unharmed.

He noticed walls around him and saw an old radio sitting in the corner of the cement room. "I'm back in Mr. Smith's cellar." He looked up, hoping to exit from the hole his body created, but it was now sealed up.

He floated off the ground, surprised that he retained his powers from the afterlife. He tried to fly upward, but the cement withstood his augmented power.

He fell back to the ground. "God put me in this cellar as punishment." Blackheart battered the walls with tremendous force, shaking the ground above but not budging the cement. He was stuck here indefinitely. He had been cast down from heaven by the Almighty and stuck in his own personal hell.

"I'm supposed to learn my lesson like this," he yelled out to God. "You're just like Smith, locking me in here. And I won't make the same mistake again. I won't wait you out and give you that same courtesy. This is war."

He punched the ground, hearing the same quiet that had plagued him when he pleaded for help when he was Mr. Smith's imprisoned victim. He stood up, realizing he had now survived the wrath of God. He had seen His worst. *I'm not afraid of challenging Him anymore.* And Blackheart would find a way back to heaven on his own terms. He slumped down in the corner next to the radio, which somehow still worked.

4

Lucerne Lake

Robert Levitan, Meadowsville's chief environmental health specialist, pulled up to Lucerne Lake, which lay on the eastern side of Meadowsville. *I'm required to continue monitoring the offensive sulfur odor exuding from the body of water.* Over the past year, by the request of the town council and many of the nearby residents, he'd filed ongoing reports.

He would submit the latest one to the council shortly. *I'll continue to explain that it's becoming increasingly dangerous.*

This often happened after a prolonged and precipitation-laden winter, which Meadowsville had experienced over the previous two years.

As the snow melted, it carried plant life and soil into the water. More plant life grew at the bottom of the lake; as it died, the decaying portions were eaten up by bacteria in the water, and they emitted hydrogen sulfide gas as a by-product. *That builds up until it reaches the air above the water and brings about the resulting rotten egg odor.* If this process continued without proper stabilization, it could prove deadly for the wildlife and hazardous for the community. *My recommendations to the township administration have been continually put off.* This was no doubt due to budget restrictions, which made him unable to properly do his job.

He would have a beer every night when he got home from work. *Just like we ignored Mr. Smith all those years—wait until this gets beyond our control. Then we can flounder and try to fix it.* His concern was for the residents and wildlife around the lake, not for the council or administration.

Levitan observed the murky fog lingering over the water, along with the whitish residue that lay on top of the lake from the chemical reactions occurring. He took out a positive-pressure demand self-contained breathing apparatus, to avoid inhaling or being exposed to the gas. He put on gloves and got out of the truck.

"No time like the present," he muttered to himself.

He walked around the edges of the lake and peered into the nearby woods, feeling the pebbles and sand crushing underneath his work boots. He noted there were somehow no dead fish or traces of any other animals, almost as if they knew the water was contaminated.

How is this possible? There should be bunches of fish floating around by now.

He looked to the trees, hoping to see squirrels or any movement, but there was nothing. It was eerily quiet all around the lake.

He wrote down his observations, noting that aeration might be an option but a call to the local EPA or branch of the Department of Natural Resources might be warranted. The putrid smell was only getting stronger, and the gas being emitted might potentially reach a flammable level. Unable to sit with his building guilt, he also jotted down that the area would need to be quarantined until they could develop a proper plan to treat the water, even just as a precaution.

The nearest houses are at least half a mile away, so they're not an immediate concern. But he still wanted to be sure no one hung around this area and suffered any potential health consequences. It was the only thing in his power to do.

He walked around the water for a little longer but saw nothing else remarkable. As he reached the half hour capacity of his breathing apparatus, he went back into the truck.

"What in God's name is going on here?" he wondered.

5

Pre-Shift Meeting

T hat night at the Meadowsville Police Department, Christian stood at his polished mahogany podium, speaking to a team of very young police officers. After the events of a year ago, Mayor Wiggins decided it was necessary to establish this new subdivision of the police department, aimed at preventing and managing supernatural events. This division had some detractors in town, but they were few, and a strong majority understood the need for such a force to be present.

Christian had been everyone's pick to lead this division, thanks to his heroism and continued due diligence protecting the town. Because the more senior officers already had experience with Blackheart, they were exempt from this program and allowed to stay on their assigned tours. The very few new officers had come out of the academy a few weeks ago and would be in this division for an entire year before progressing to ride-alongs with the senior officers on regular street duty and then to being out on their own. What would ideally be ten new officers was only half a dozen, due to the township's budget restrictions. The new contract these officers were hired under saw many perks removed, such as free healthcare after retirement, and they now had to put in thirty years in before getting their pensions.

"So your advanced directives are as follows," Christian said to the group, pointing to a whiteboard with several tasks written on them. "The resident at 667 Anemone Road put in an anonymous message about having their spotlights going off every night. No animal tracks or anything. Their security cameras caught some shadows but nothing concrete. Give it at least one to two drive-bys each night for now."

Some of officers took pictures of the address with their smart phones while others wrote in tiny little notepads that they stored in their breast pockets.

"Check Chrysanthemum Drive at least once. And please, do a perimeter check on foot. You don't have to spend an hour there, but make sure nothing is disturbed. If it is, you know the drill . . . call me ASAP so I can come out."

One of the officers raised his hand. The name *Cyders* sparkled off of his crisp badge that had not seen even a single speck of dust, let alone any action at this point in his short career.

Christian looked away from the board and nodded at him to speak.

"Sir, if I can speak freely, is this stuff for real? Seems like all we're doing is chasing shadows and spooky noises."

A few of the other officers chuckled and looked down, trying to hide their expressions. While Christian was medicated and calmer these days, hearing such ignorance brought him back to the Meadowsville that he grew up in. The town that oozed resistance to change, even at the expense of its citizens at the hands of the monsters that once roamed the streets.

Christian displayed an exaggerated, cantankerous smile and left his podium, slowly walking toward the young man. He looked out the window of the police station at the night sky. There was no moon or stars visible on the slightly cloudy night. Christian thought back to wearing his armor and working alone. Part of him missed it, but he fully recognized that he was not in his right mind at the time. Having his family as a loving, cohesive unit meant more to him than any town patrol or suit of armor. He turned his attention back to the question directed at him.

"Officer Cyders," he said calmly. "You're new to this town, aren't you?"

Cyders nodded, watching Christian intently, as did the other officers. They were unsure if he would just dress Cyders down a bit or take a swing at him for the obnoxious question.

"And you've heard about the strange stuff that's gone down in the last few decades?"

Cyders nodded again.

"Let me rattle off a few truths out to you about Meadowsville. We ignored little things for a long time and they became big problems. We've lost thousands of residents, including my daughter and my parents, and there's been so much damage done to the town itself that it's gonna take us a very long time to fix it all up."

"Sir, I didn't mean—"

Christian cut him off. "I used to be like you. Young and dumb. Even after my parents were murdered in front of me. I assumed it was just a random crime, exaggerated by a little kid who witnessed it, or something more reasonable, because I wasn't ready to absorb the truth that was in front of my eyes. And I fell in line with the other people of this town and became passive. Because the problems were always debunked with some false cause or whatever else to protect the financial interests of the higher-ups here. And I grew up in the care of my relatives here, who are luckily deceased of natural causes now and didn't suffer at the hands of the monsters that used to roam free. I married my beautiful wife and had two kids and attempted to raise my family, trying to live in a town full of lies, hopeful that I'd never have to see the sheer ugliness of this place ever again. And then reality punched me right in the fuckin' mouth when it killed my daughter right front of me." Christian sneered, punching the wall above Cyders, leaving a small dent and making all the officers jump.

Christian looked at his knuckle, which showed no damage, and he felt no pain. He smiled, thinking back to punching Blackheart during the town's anniversary celebration, hitting him hard enough to kill some of nerves in the hand, but it had been worth it.

Cyders attempted to speak, but Christian put his finger up to silence him. The other officers appeared uncomfortable, watching the interaction.

"There's a lot we don't know about the things that happened. Those creatures. But I was there to save this place several times. I did battle and risked my life. That's why I have so much arthritis that I can barely move in any way without some degree of pain. But you know what? I wear this pain and these injuries like medals of honor. You can thank not only me but a select few others out there who made it possible for you to be here right now."

Christian motioned for Cyders to stand up, and when he complied, Christian came within a few inches of the officer's face. He noticed the beads of sweat now coming off the man's temple and the slight quiver of his bottom lip as he fumbled the gum in his mouth.

"All we can do is give you some exposure to what's happened and try to educate you on what we do know. For this town's protection. For you, your loved ones, friends, and colleagues. You are police officers to serve the people and maintain order. Sometimes you may have to think outside the box of your formal training. Things that aren't taught to you in the academy or out of some textbook. But once you leave this division, you should be confident enough to handle anything you encounter. Whether a carjacker, a drunk, or even a monster. Welcome to Meadowsville, rookie. Now pull up your pants and fall in line."

Officer Cyders stood still, humbled and slightly rattled by Christian, who went back to his podium, limping a little, from the chronic pain in the hip that Blackheart fractured last year.

"Now, are there any other questions before you guys hit the road?"

No one raised their hand. Christian began tossing keys for the police cruisers at each officer, writing down who was assigned to what car.

"Make sure your body cameras are on, and I'll be watching the GPS on each of your vehicles. If I see anyone idling for more than one hour, I will assume you're sleeping and will come out to wake you up. Now get out there and be safe. Call in if you need anything. I'll be here all night."

The officers quickly scampered out of the room. None of them said anything to each other about the tense pre-shift lineup.

Christian sat, beginning another long night of his shift. There were rarely any calls from his team, and even if he fell asleep, the radio woke him right up. His cell phone lit up from a funny cartoon Rebecca sent him. It was an old man getting swallowed by a toilet, headfirst, and read, "Bottoms up."

She has the same twisted sense of humor that I do. He replied with a smile emoji, and they wished each other good night.

Christian walked around the near empty police department, listening to the dispatchers take calls a few rooms over. He admired the various plaques of the officers who died during Blackheart's attacks over the last sixteen years. The newly renovated police department looked great, and it was an honor to be a part of it.

He fought a sense of regret that he could have done more to save those fallen officers but quickly realized he'd given too much as it was. He took his phone out again and looked at a picture of his family, back when Caroline was alive and Adam was still a baby. He smiled at the sight of his two beautiful children and his wife, who continued to be his best friend and emotional crutch. Even after all this time, he still greatly missed Caroline, as did Rebecca and Adam. They visited her grave each Sunday before attending Alexandra's service—and on Caroline's birthday and holidays too. They were all somber visits, but with all three of the remaining family members there, they would joke and laugh sometimes, interacting with Caroline's grave-stone as if it were actually her.

His phone alarm went off, and he took his one antidepressant.

6

Renewed Faith

The next morning, Alexandra Hughes sat in her newly renovated church. The repaired stained glass windows shone brightly and illuminated the freshly polished pews and altar furnishings. She looked around, remembering her father showing her how he would arrange his sermon notes each week, the two of them finding David in pieces the first time he came there, and then Blackheart, with his hypnotizing gaze, staring right through her. This house of worship was chock-full of memories she cherished and others she wished never happened.

Since the events with Blackheart last year, the town saw the strength and courage Alexandra possessed. They flocked to her in such great volumes that, on certain days, people would stand outside and listen in from the open windows. She even had to start offering services six days a week to keep up with the demand. While exhausting, she could handle the schedule and had more residents offering to help her do upkeep on the church and manage her time.

As this occurred, town-wide her colleagues had become very resistant toward working with her to create a more cohesive religious movement in town. They had all shied away from her, mostly from losing so many of their members to her church. Alex had even developed some ideas and plans to push people back into their former places of worship, but that was also met with some indignation. Rumors swirled that the other leaders felt like this was a pity tactic, meant to offer charity, strongly insinuating she felt they needed her help to operate. The mixed feelings were just a source of frustration to Alex, but she continued to do outreach as much as possible in hopes that they one day would come around to working with her. She was thankful each and every day for the few colleagues who were still open to speaking with her.

She looked at the spot where she had laid Blackheart to rest and remembered the feeling of being both humbled and prideful. How could she put down an immortal creature like that but couldn't wrangle together a few dozen religious leaders? *Frustrating, to say the least.*

"God, please hear my words and prayers. I look to you for guidance and support. Please help me reach the others. Give me a sign or anything that I can use to bring them together. We are no match for any future dangers unless we are united."

She looked to the stained glass window of Jesus and hoped to hear him speak down to her, but it wouldn't happen. She waited on the leaders of every house of worship in Meadowsville. The silence ate at her psyche. She sat down, losing hope of every person arriving but knowing she had to keep her thoughts grounded in reality. Suddenly, seven of her attendees came in. They were fewer in number than she had hoped for, but she had to make do with what she had at her disposal nowadays. She perked up as they politely greeted her and took seats. All of them were dressed in neatly put together suits. The circle of them resembled an executive meeting, not one concerning congregations. No one spoke, so Alex took the lead, not acknowledging that her blouse and long skirt made her feel a bit underdressed.

"Thank you for coming, everyone."

"Alexandra, the others won't be coming today," Father Nicolas of Holy Name Catholic Church said.

"Thank you for confirming that. So we can begin."

"Why have you asked us here?" Reverend Damien Graham of the United Reformed Church asked.

"Because things are not where they should be. And you already know that. There is great dissention among us, and that cannot stand. It is our obligation to keep this town on a clear spiritual path to avoid any further dissention. After all the biblical things we've seen in recent memory, it's up to us to keep the spirituality of this entire town as strong as possible. And we can't do that apart. Only together."

"That may be. But we have another bigger problem. You've poached so many of our members. It's hurt our churches very badly. We've all taken pay cuts and had to reduce the budgets in our houses of worship. That's directly hurt our remaining members too. And I, for one, am not looking for a handout. I want to have a partnership with your church that evens things out once again," Pastor Andrew Morris of the Grace United Presbyterian chimed in.

"And I apologize for that. I preached for months how people should not look to me as the sole religious leader in the town. I urged them to return to your houses of worship to hear your words so we could all be unified as one under God. All unique and special in His eyes, but unified nonetheless."

"But it didn't work. They all stayed here," Father Nicolas added. "They've ignored our outreach."

"I can't force people to return," Alex said, becoming defensive. "I've tried everything I could think of."

"I will agree with you that there has been a fair amount of spiritual laxity that has come over Meadowsville in the last several months. And that is a big problem we must all combat. And we are willing to work with you, but unfortunately, things are bigger than just eight people. There are dozens of others who need to be with us to make such a movement work, but they're not interested. They need to be a part of this conversation. Without all of us here together, this and any further meetings are useless," Pastor Andrew Taylor of Meadowsville Methodist Church added.

"What can we do to convince them otherwise?" Alex asked. "I've called, emailed, and even showed up in person, but it's not working. The others are closed off."

"I don't know. This town has patterns that it seems to just be content abiding by. It only seems to flock to God when something scares them bad enough. But even after that, they return to passive faith again. Like they view God as an insurance policy. Only useful in emergencies. I don't know if there needs to be a big enough event that permanently alters that habit, if that's even possible after last year with that demon, or if it's up to us to do a better job of retaining them. Could be either. But it's very complex," Reverend Rupert Martin of Meadowsville Baptist Church said.

Alex remembered Blackheart dying in front of her again, hoping that was the end of the plagues that had been bestowed upon Meadowsville. This meeting assured her that it wasn't. She knew it, as did all of the other leaders. It was just a matter of when, not if, something bad would happen. The lack of faith in their community was a big, open, festering wound. She and Christian had spoken of the possibility of John Smith's body being dug up during the potential Chrysanthemum Drive remediation, which gave her a sinking feeling that Meadowsville was primed for another large-scale problem.

"Faith is the strongest weapon we have. God will always prevail. No matter what. We just need to make sure the residents here all realize that, as we all do. Keep God fresh in their minds, so they don't stray like this. So they don't look to false idols like Mr. Smith or Blackheart ever again," Alex told the group, who all agreed. "I think we all need to use our own connections to our fellow places of worship to get everyone together once again. They may not want to hear from me, but they'll listen to all of us as a united front. From there, we keep building and working on this initiative together; we can then focus on reconnecting everyone to our individual churches and to Him."

The small group continued to discuss their options and agreed they needed to bring the spiritual guidance of Meadowsville back to an adequate level. If not, they would be susceptible to another major difficulty that could be apocalyptic in nature.

7

Mr. Smith

Blackheart listened to the radio, slumped in a corner, as it projected static-filled and broken up songs—

Teach them your way
Don't let them get away

It had been several days since he had been condemned to this prison with no way out. Blackheart looked at the front right corner of the room, where he used his overgrown fingernails as a child and carved his name, *Timothy*, into the cement. This aided him in avoiding the mental anguish during the time of abuse and turmoil at Smith's hands. The name he had spent so long distancing himself from. The name that died with John Smith, the abuser who died of natural causes and never saw justice for the atrocities he committed against so many people.

The carving took years and served as a way to pass the time. After a while, his fingers stopped hurting and as he got closer to each letter being completed, he felt increasingly satisfied. He would bleed from his nail beds and lick off the blood, but Smith would beat him if he saw. Smith wanted him to feed by killing others, not use himself. His attempt to use his own blood showed weakness, a lack of self-sufficiency, and an inability to learn what Smith was forcing on him. Just like with God, he was again being punished for not conforming to a set of standards.

Blackheart briefly remembered David, who had the same issue with being unable to kill. Blackheart tried so hard to get David to learn how to exist as a vampire. David could have succeeded where Blackheart had failed, all if he'd taken better direction. But that was in the past. Blackheart was acutely aware that he had evolved into some kind of deity and grew increasingly less concerned about his past dealings.

Blackheart began to think more about the time he spent with Smith—the decades Blackheart was held prisoner in this place. No one could hear his screams as Smith brutalized him and ripped every bit of innocence away. He recalled trying desperately trying to grab something to fight him off with during each attack but to no avail. Smith ruled over him, just as God was doing now. The same God that had cast Blackheart down, restricting him to the dirty cement cellar. It was a despicable abuse of authority by the highest power in existence.

Blackheart had never been able to kill Smith for all his misdeeds, but he stood a chance to combat God and never be a victim ever again. Blackheart had the abilities and a vicious streak of resentment in order to see this through. He was so close to achieving his destiny of challenging God, and He knew it. That's why Blackheart was sent back to earth. God was scared of Blackheart's potential in the heavens. That was why He kept Blackheart in the serene field, in what he assumed was heaven, all that time. He didn't want Blackheart to see anything beyond that for fear of somehow losing His place on the throne. God tried to keep Blackheart like an obedient pet, just like Smith did.

They can hear you from beyond the grave
Make them all your slaves

Blackheart heard the broken lyrics from the radio, and it made him think of John Smith again. The thoughts of Smith's ugly smile, the feeling of the monster's hot breath on his hair, and the cold hands exploring his young body. The memories felt like a jackhammer in his mind.

He then recalled that Smith's body was still buried near the cellar. Blackheart had been the one who buried him and then placed the gravestone in the Meadowsville Community Church cemetery. He carved the entire nameplate with his nails, just as he did with his own name on the cellar wall.

Blackheart thought back to all the people's dreams he had entered during his previous tenure on earth: David, Alexandra, and a myriad of others. It was a way to connect with the individuals of interest to him and begin the process of grooming them all to fall subservient. And the manipulation through dreams never failed—Alexandra was the only exception. Blackheart then wondered whether he could enter John Smith's mind, if it was still viable, so he could use him to somehow get him out of this prison.

He came up with a scenario where he could resurrect Smith to bring about a level of destruction to Meadowsville and then beyond the town. The people would feel true fear of Smith once again as he would rape their children, murder whomever he pleased, and create the long-forgotten atmosphere of total fear. This would put the town's faith back in Blackheart to save them from the unhinged beast, as they would not be able to defend themselves, much like during Smith's prime. Blackheart knew the power and longevity of Smith, and the citizens of Meadowsville would not be able to destroy him on their own. They would panic and resort to the evil they knew in him. They would think of Blackheart, and it would spread like wildfire. Their thoughts and energy would give him the necessary power to break out of the cement box he was stuck in. He would then easily dispatch Smith, and the world would be ripe for him to rule over.

They would all worship him—not unlike before but now as a legitimate divine spirit. He would be viewed as their savior who was brought back to rescue them, requiring only their faith and love. Once that was accomplished, he would front a hostile takeover. He would accomplish all his goals in rapid fashion. He would make the people of Meadowsville pay for allowing him to be abused by John Smith all those years ago.

Then he would destroy their town and anyone who didn't worship him. He would expand beyond, doing the same to everyone else on earth. And as the billions of people bowed before him, his power would be godlike, as their praises would feed him and increase his abilities. And once he had the world under his control, he would be so charged up with power that he could then challenge God and hopefully succeed Him. He would use God's greatest creation against him. Blackheart would never be victimized again.

> *Angels sent crashing down*
> *God just letting them drown*

Blackheart silenced his thoughts and entered a deep, quiet state of being. He had only to concentrate and keep an image of the person in his mind in order to enter their psyche. And with his newfound abilities, it was easier than he remembered. He allowed all his heightened energy to locate the body of John Smith, which was no more than a few feet away from him, past the dirt and cement walls of the cellar.

He asked, *"Do you smell the offering I made to you? Is the odor of those children from a year ago still strong and to your liking?"*

There was nothing at first, but then Blackheart sensed some form of a strengthened connection. While Smith had died of old age, the combination of Blackheart's blood being shed into the soil last year as he battled Christian, the smell of the children, and the power of Blackheart's psychological invasion had resurrected Smith, even just slightly. Blackheart smiled ear to ear and realized his plan would work. It had to.

Smith became more viable as Blackheart continued speaking to him.

"Do you want to taste my blood? The blood of a god? The blood of the only child victim you never tasted?"

Smith preferred to poison Blackheart only through brutal sexual assaults.

Smith opened his eyes slightly, but the dirt weighed him down, leaving him unable to do anything in his weakened state. He licked his vile lips, tasting a single drop of Blackheart's blood hidden in the particles of dirt. It was far from pure, but it was enough to exhibit a response. Smith regained a slight sense of smell, which made him become sexually aroused by the year-old odor of the frightened children, which still lingered from the cement cellar.

You can't be outrun
The end has begun

Blackheart continued feeding Smith the memories of his past victims and visions of each time he was raped as a child, bringing Smith closer to becoming alive once again.

He continued the neural onslaught for days . . .

8

Controversial Decision

Meadowsville Town Council meeting was already underway. Mayor Wiggins sat with his four council members—Andrews, Brown, Johnson, and Miller—facing the crowd.

"And I promise that the issues with Lucerne Lake are being looked into," the mayor stated. "Mr. Levitan is working closely with officials on this matter. We agree with his opinion, and the area is officially quarantined. Please do not go past the barriers, even if just walking your dogs. And don't think of letting your kids swim in it. The smell is awful, and that should remind you to stay away from it. It's not safe, so please stay away."

The crowd grumbled a bit but settled quickly.

"On to the budget. We are increasing our profit margin, but unfortunately, due to the damage from the incidents last year and the rushed mandatory repairs to the MPD and MFD buildings, along with the MPS program initiation, we are back in the red again," Wiggins continued, swallowing hard but forcing himself to never lie to the town ever again. "Not just in the red but drowning in the red."

The crowd stayed silent, but a few sighs were heard.

"We have discussed several options and want your feedback. We either raise taxes, furlough staff members of the township indefinitely, working with only skeleton crews, or we find a new way to bring tourism back."

"What about rebuilding the house on Chrysanthemum Drive?" Councilman Andrews said.

Everyone in the room turned in complete silence and looked at him in utter disbelief.

"What! Is this some kind of sick joke?" Christian yelled, standing up, losing his patience. Despite being privy to the concept prior, hearing it said out loud to everyone stirred a nasty reaction. It was *real* now.

"Councilman Andrews, could you clarify your suggestion for the audience?" the mayor asked, already aware of the idea.

"Well . . . um . . . we need profits up, and any idea we come up with will be an educated guess. But if you review the past financials when our tourism *was* up, we know that people like the mystique and appeal of a creature in this town. Look at other places in the world with longstanding traditions involving things like the Loch Ness monster and Bigfoot. It sells and keeps their economies going strong," Andrews said cautiously. "Smith, Blackheart . . . doesn't matter what it is, just as long as there is actually something here that represents the supernatural. And unlike their monsters, ours have been proven to exist."

"You shouldn't touch the land," Christian yelled from the audience. "John Smith's body is still in there somewhere. And God knows what else. We don't know enough about these creatures, and until we do, it's not safe. We don't know what'll happen. It's not worth the risk."

"I have to agree. I have given this some thought lately, and I just don't think it's a good idea," Wiggins agreed. "What if we marketed something about Lucerne Lake? Add a bit of the mystique here. It's quarantined, and we know what the problem is, and it can be managed. Maybe say it's haunted by the ghost of . . ." He stopped short of saying John Smith's name.

No one in the crowd responded.

"Chrysanthemum represents death. That's exactly what you're going to get if you play around on that property," Christian interjected again.

The audience sat contemplating such an extreme concept.

"I'm not saying to glorify or open ourselves up to any more problems, but last year's incidents are still fresh in everyone's minds. We can capitalize on that," Andrews continued.

"And we could make a tasteful memorial for all the victims too," Councilwoman Miller added in, coming on board. "Could be a great PR move for us too. Mayor Wiggins, I know that was an initiative you originally brought up, so this could all work out for everyone."

Christian and Mayor Wiggins locked eyes, both displeased by this growing movement.

Wiggins continually felt awful for even suggesting this to the council earlier, and both men had immense fear of where this would all end up. As the rumblings in the crowd grew, it showed the group completely split on the matter. The council members covered their microphones and spoke among themselves as the meeting was taken out of Mayor Wiggins's control. He quickly searched for some way to willingly support this idea, knowing it would be a guaranteed profitable venture, but he didn't want to. He was so very concerned over the safety issues at play. With the common knowledge of how he tried to hide Blackheart's resurrection last year, he had lost a good deal of support and desperately wanted to regain it.

"No one should have to lose money. Not by increased taxes or reduced paychecks. You've all been through plenty living here," Councilman Brown interjected. "I support this motion. Let's build the house and promote it. Build it just the way it was."

"Okay, okay. Everyone in favor," Mayor Wiggins called out, closing his eyes, not able to look at Christian's desperate and fearful face, hoping that a majority of the attendees rejected it.

A slim majority of the crowd raised their hands. Some appeared questionable, but all understood the reasoning for this motion.

Wiggins then called for the unfavorable voters, who were in the minority.

"Motion passes. Construction to begin ASAP. I will accept vendor bids from the council and approve the most reasonable quotes," he declared, unenthused.

Once the gavel struck, the audience finally realized what has just been agreed upon. The room became filled with arguments between the two opposing sides, and Mayor Wiggins tried to calm their fears as best he could. The division in the town was starting again, and this made them all more prone and vulnerable. This was not how Wiggins wanted this meeting to turn out. He considered trying to leave the room but stopped himself abruptly and forced himself back in.

"However," Wiggins began, drowning out all the other noise in the room, "I am going to pass an additional mandate that Christian and his team will patrol the grounds multiple times per night and also be in constant contact with the construction workers. If anything happens that is out of the ordinary, I will shut down the project without so much as a second thought."

Christian and the mayor finally locked eyes again, both feeling a strong level of dread over what has just been done.

9

History Lesson

I n Meadowsville High School, Adam sat in his modern world history course. It was a small class of about fifteen students, all seated comfortably in a circular pattern of desks. Some students had their feet on the desks, and others were texting on their phones. When Mr. Edmonson spoke, however, everyone listened. He ran a very relaxed learning environment, and all he demanded was a common respect among his students and for them to follow his instruction. None of the students took issue with that, especially Adam, who preferred a less structured class.

Mr. Edmonson started calling out names of various students who would each would be responsible for presenting a minimum ten-page research project next month to the class, in teams of two.

"Jake and . . . Josh. Jayden and Jamie. Jack and Jill."

Everyone began moving their seats to be alongside their designated partners, and Adam remained uncalled.

"Adam and Bruce."

Both boys looked at each other with a tense stare. They had not had much contact with each another after their incident last year.

Adam moved his chair next to Bruce but remained a few feet away as they looked at one another carefully. Adam noticed the small scar on the left side of Bruce's forehead from when he beat him with that piece of locker last year. Since that fight, Bruce had left Adam alone and stopped his barrage of teases and taunts. Between besting Bruce during their fight and seeing firsthand what a true hero Christian was, he quickly became humbled toward Adam.

"Guess it's you and me, kid," Bruce said, showing a civil side that was normally unrecognizable to Adam.

"Looks that way," Adam said slowly, cautiously moving closer to Bruce.

"Hey, I'm sorry if I gave you a hard time last year," Bruce carefully put across.

Adam sat, completely at a loss for words. "Um, yeah, it's no big deal. Water under the bridge."

"How's your dad been?"

"Uh, okay, I guess," Adam replied, still feeling out the interaction. "He's a little banged up but hangin' in."

Bruce nodded, subtly expressing his new respect of Mr. Reed, and asked, "So, what topic off the list do you wanna cover?"

They both read the list, which included the Franco-Spanish War, the American Civil War, and the Crusades. Neither said anything and sat in silence as their classmates all seemed to choose easily and discuss their topics with Mr. Edmonson.

"I actually had a different idea," Adam said.

"Like what?" Bruce inquired.

"What if we developed a brief history of the town as it related to Mr. Smith and Blackheart and such? I don't think anyone else has tackled it yet. Anything written is all from these unconfirmed sources or has been made up to embellish what was actually happening to sell books. But no one has actually tried to piece it all together. We could give it a shot."

Bruce sat back in his chair and laced his hands behind his head, looking up at the ceiling. "It's definitely interesting," he replied, still thinking on it.

Mr. Edmonson approached the two, knowing their prior rivalry. He was glad to see no one had thrown a desk or put the other person in a headlock.

"So, what's it gonna be, boys?" he asked, leaning on the nearby wall, crossing his hairy arms.

"Well, I had an idea for our research project," Adam put out.

"Sure, Adam, let's have it," Edmonson quickly asked. "Bruce, this okay with you?"

Bruce nodded.

Adam presented his idea. "We'd like to attempt to piece together the town's history through when Smith and then Blackheart came into the picture. Even like the founding families and all that."

"Smith was a founding member of the town. So how did he go from that to what he became, abducting little kids and killing people," Bruce added in, remembering Mayor Wiggins stating that fact at town's anniversary celebration last year.

"Well, you've both got my curiosity. It's a big idea. Still a lot of conversation over what happened throughout the years. You have your dad to consult with too," Edmonson said. "But I'm really intrigued by what you could do with a project like this. But, again, you two need to do a good job with this. I don't want to hear anything from the other towns with their conspiracy theories or any of that, okay? I want you going through the available history and put together what you can. And if you can't connect anything directly, you can make some educated guesses, but I want to hear the thought process toward your deductions. Is that all fair?"

Both boys agreed.

"I feel like this could be the start of an accurate history of the town. No more bullshit," Bruce jumped in.

Edmonson smiled and looked at his freshly shined loafers, not caring about the curse. He was elated to see the boys working together and genuinely excited to do work on a project of this magnitude.

"Well, if you guys want it, you have my blessing—" He stopped and became a bit anxious. "Wait, don't tell anyone I said that. The principal doesn't like teachers bringing religion into the classroom. It's a newer policy that he's put into place this year and enforcing hard with the staff. I don't know why. Bad choice of words on my part."

Mr. Edmonson let out a long exhalation and looked at Adam and Bruce, who weren't sure how to proceed.

"Moving on . . . yes, I like the idea and love your enthusiasm. Keep in mind that this is going to be a significant portion of your grade for this year. And both of you get the same grade, no matter if one person does more work than the other. The assignment means something, but I want to see equal work from both sides and a solid demonstration of teamwork. So you guys need to be sure of what you want to do."

Adam and Bruce looked at it other and shook hands on it.

"Okay, have at it," Mr. Edmonson said, waddling away a bit, still embarrassed by his gaffe.

As the bell rang shortly after to dismiss class, Bruce and Adam walked out of the classroom. Bruce was much bigger than Adam, now being a senior, so they resembled a big brother walking his younger sibling. Adam was floored that Bruce had developed this much respect for someone who he bullied for years, up until their fight last year. They managed to avoid one another since that incident, but now they were working together as a team.

A senior bumped into Adam purposefully, knocking him into some lockers.

"Sorry, Reed," the boy called out sarcastically.

Bruce grabbed the aggressor's backpack and pulled him backward, away from the three classmates he was walking with. He quickly redirected the boy back to Adam. "I think you meant to say you were sorry. And mean it this time."

The boy seemed angry and didn't say anything, trying to get away. Bruce stopped the boy's resistance and pushed him harder toward Adam, overpowering him.

"This isn't hard. Tell my buddy you're sorry."

"I'm sorry," the boy said before shaking off Bruce.

Adam enjoyed watching Bruce torment a bully, further proving his change of heart toward his once bitter rival. "So you're slumming with the babies now, Fuller?"

"Something like that," Bruce replied, ready to fight the boy.

Mr. Edmonson stood in the hallway watching, and Adam now noticed his presence. He patted Bruce on the shoulder and got him away from the scene before anyone got in trouble. Edmonson was thrilled that Bruce and Adam were now cordial with one another.

Bruce shook off the ordeal and continued walking with Adam.

As the two boys walked down the hall, Bruce noticed Adam checking out fellow senior Bonnie Slater's legs sticking out of a very short skirt.

"Some stems on that girl, huh?" He joked to Adam, getting him to crack a smile.

Any residual tension seemed to diminish in that moment.

As the boys walked down the hall, they passed an aged set of class pictures hung on the wall, from almost twenty years ago, showing David and his best friend, Erik, making funny faces at the camera. What were once two energetic but troubled youths had been lost, like so many others, to Blackheart.

10

Unenthused Approval

Mayor Wiggins sat alone in his office, looking at the estimates for the mansion reconstruction. *I'm not comfortable at the idea of playing with such a sensitive subject in Meadowsville's history.* He also understood that if this was what the people wanted, he needed to lead them a certain way.

He was confident in Christian overseeing the protection detail but realized his reelection campaign, set for later in the year, could no longer be focused on ignoring the creatures that once inhabited the town. He was embellishing them for profit. He felt disappointed that he had somehow let the town down by approving the work to be done.

"Three million to remediate the soil. Two million to clean up and dispose of the wreckage. Two million to rebuild the mansion. My God," he said to himself. "And three hundred forty thousand a year for operating expenses!"

He tossed the paperwork onto the floor across his office and saw a copy of today's *Meadowsville Quill* newspaper with the front headline reading, "Sensible or Crazy? What is Wiggins Going to Do?"

"I have no choice. I'm going to have to renegotiate all the contracts, cut off all the vendors, and lay off workers to make this happen. I'm overruled here."

He turned his head, now looking at the portraits of his predecessors. He came to Mayor Wilkins and remembered Blackheart throwing her beaten and bloodied corpse onto him at the town's anniversary. Her face was withered and drained of everything. He wondered if it was from the years of massive corruption she had been overseeing, the stress from the job as mayor, or the creature that burdened her for her entire political career. Or maybe it was from all of it.

"I can't let myself become like her. I just can't," he said to himself. "But what am I supposed to do?"

He folded his hands, resting his chin on them. He looked at the email chain from the town council, all the messages hounding him to authorize approval to begin work on Chrysanthemum Drive. He then looked at a fresh message from his public relations lead, showing he was in danger of losing a lion's share of his voters if he didn't see this project through.

He rubbed his eyes vigorously and slammed his hand down on the desk. He was stuck and had to approve the work. He reasoned that if anyone else got elected mayor, whether an outsider or lifelong resident, they could put Meadowsville into a very dire situation. They wouldn't put as much thought and consideration into something like this, as he did. They would possibly be no better than Mayor Wilkins, just doing whatever was necessary to make a profit. Exposing the citizens to unimaginable terrors and risks.

Wiggins sat, conflicted on how to proceed with everything, to balance it all. His pure intentions and drive to do things the right way made him the best person to lead Meadowsville. He would have to bend to this decision in order to keep himself in that position of power. And once the dust settled, he would do everything in his power to control it all and bring the town to a more profitable and untarnished place.

He looked at a picture of his wife, Eleanor. "I'm glad we weren't able to conceive children." Neither one of them had the ability to do so.

But he was thankful for not having to look his children in the face and tell them everything would be okay in their town. It wasn't honest, and he wouldn't have been able to do it. But again, he had to make a move—and then worry about potential complications later.

"If you can't beat it, then might as well join it," he conceded.

He picked up the paperwork to authorize construction and signed it.

"I hope this isn't as big a mistake as I think it is," he said, almost shedding a tear, fearful of what would happen.

He stayed in his office for another hour, looking out the picture window at the quiet town. All of the children, older adults, working class and every other type of resident, depended on him to do what was best. He then wondered how everything came back to this again. Like the town was afraid to move on, as if there were still another devastating chapter to tell before there was full closure for Meadowsville.

11

Unearthing Evil

Several days later, bulldozers, tractors, dump trucks, and other construction vehicles sat atop Chrysanthemum Drive. The dozens of teamsters sipped their coffee and gabbed for almost two hours after arriving early that morning. As they began to work, some of the workers tossed their empty cups and cigarette butts into the dirt. Like a well-orchestrated production, one team began pushing the house remnants into a big pile, preparing it to be lifted and removed by the dump trucks. Another team began remediating the dirt on the solid acre of land, piling the dirt into other trucks to be disposed of. The third and last team stayed on the outskirts of the property, cutting down the dead trees and branches from Blackheart's last escapade.

John Smith continued to lie in his suspended state of unconsciousness. He'd been buried for almost seventy-five years. Due to dying of natural causes, he was mostly intact aside from some degeneration from the passing time and the bugs living inside his body. Now, with Blackheart's telepathic messages, the tiny bit of his lasting energy was revived. The sweet remnants of Blackheart's blood in the dirt brought him back physically too. There was something in Blackheart's blood that was different than other vampires' essence. It had rejuvenating properties that could bring about new life.

Smith, below many feet of dirt and debris, felt the vibration of the equipment above. He regained more and more of his memory as Blackheart continued sending Smith horrible thoughts of violence and torture, all of which had actually happened. Blackheart made sure it involved the hundreds of times he had raped Blackheart as a child or made him watch people be murdered in cold blood. Blackheart cringed while trying to maintain focus on his target, but it was terribly painful and upsetting to relive all the events. He recalled calling out to God for help so many times and simply being left there—just as he was now in that cellar, once again depending on John Smith for survival. Blackheart hated himself for what he was doing, but it would allow him to fulfill his bigger plans.

Smith smiled, exposing two razor-sharp canines and allowing more tainted dirt to fill his mouth. He continued to lick the soil with Blackheart's blood residue in it. After a few more hours, he eventually licked the bits of remaining skin off his lips and jostled it around his few remaining teeth. The teamsters continued working above, and each dig at the foundation of the property not only rejuvenated Smith but allowed him increasingly better movement.

Within a week, the property was cleaned out, the land was remediated, and the rebuilding began to construct the house exactly as it had been. The workers left the cement cellar intact, not knowing of Blackheart's presence in it, as it was also a part of the original floor plans and appeared in perfect condition from the outside. They also couldn't access the inside of it, nor could it be removed, as if some force were keeping it there.

12

Shaken Faith

Alexandra found herself in a nightmare.

A bright blue sky with a staircase made of clouds seemed to lead into the sun. Somehow, it didn't hurt her eyes as she looked directly into it. She climbed it, feeling totally at peace. She wasn't able to see God but felt his presence all around her. It was such a unique feeling but comforting, almost similar to a loving parent's warm embrace.

As she neared the top of the stairs, God's company became drastically worrisome. She looked down, and her vision zoomed rapidly toward the ground, following a fiery object as it crashed into Blackheart's mansion. The earth shook as it landed, and a dragon emerged from the dirt. It had sickly, gnarled scale patterns and large claws on all four of its limbs. As it climbed out of the dirt, each step it made left a wake of destruction causing extraordinary firestorms. It whipped its head around, and the flames around it made the mighty horns shine. It then let out a powerful roar that flattened the entire town of Meadowsville. All the people she cared for screamed from within the fires. She began to tear up and wanted to help but was still in the clouds.

The small number of remaining citizens bowed down in submission as the dragon exposed a pair of powerful wings and took to the now blackened skies, looking down on them. It then breached the town and flew around the surrounding areas, which were still unharmed. It roared one last time, spewing a stream of fire across the entire sky, which saw the entire earth burn. A comforting hand grasped her shoulder, and she looked up to see green eyes looking back at her. She recognized those eyes. They belonged to David, and they looked worried.

She startled and awoke, sweating profusely. She rubbed her eyes to help her wake up and then wondered whether something bad had happened with the work being done on Chrysanthemum Drive. She got out of bed and quickly got herself ready for the day, which included her Sunday church service. She displaced the dream temporarily until she could process it further and speak with Christian.

She walked from her parsonage, looking at the sky, where the sun was bright as could be. There were no distressing sounds, explosions, screaming, or anything she recalled from Blackheart's previous attacks, so she felt somewhat at ease in the interim. Large groups of attendees stood around the entranceway of the church, welcoming her. She put on a fake smile and thanked them all for being there with her that day but couldn't get past the feeling of dread she had woken up with.

She went to her office and put on her vestments, praying quietly to herself again. She felt more uneasy going to the altar than she had since originally taking over the church for her father, but she tried to be strong.

As she looked out at the overflowing congregation, there was a noticeable decrease from the week prior—and the month before that. The trend that she and the other church leaders feared was truly happening. The citizens were no longer maintaining their faith and were becoming complacent with their beliefs. It was no longer a matter of everyone flocking to the Meadowsville Community Church, but now they were just starting to stop attending services altogether. She knew deep in her soul that her dream was a foreshadowing of an Armageddon-level happening. She had never dreamed of David before, but now she felt he was trying to warn her.

13

New Generation

Christian took several over-the-counter painkillers and rolled his ankles and wrists several times before wrestling Adam on the floor of the finished basement in their house. Christian put Adam in an armlock, but he was able to overpower Christian, rolling into a triangle choke maneuver. Adam had become strong, and Christian was too damaged to keep up. But one thing he'd have to further instruct his son on was not relying just on strength and power but also being smart and tactical in his approach. He could let Adam win but needed to teach him this valuable lesson.

"Come on, Pop. I thought you were supposed to be good at this," Adam joked, locking in the hold.

Christian had come to peace with Adam being able to win this round but rolled him over onto his stomach and put him into a Mexican surfboard submission. The two could get aggressive, but the majority of the time, their bouts were just friendly practice.

"I'd ask you to tap out, but you seem to have no use of your arms," Christian jabbed back at his son.

"Okay, okay, okay . . . I give," Adam said, unable to move.

Christian let go and patted him on the back. "Brute force isn't always the best path. You got so tired breaking that armlock that you couldn't keep me in the triangle lock."

"I thought I had you that time," Adam replied, panting.

"You almost did. You've learned so much and improved a ton," Christian said, using a towel to blot his sweaty forehead. "But remember to think before you act. Intelligence and cunning are your most powerful weapons, above all else."

Adam nodded out of respect for the impromptu lesson. His father had received some formal training in various fighting techniques after his initial encounter with Blackheart, and Adam appreciated the knowledge Christian had for defending himself. He grabbed a water bottle off some of the clutter in the basement and accidentally pulled a tarp onto the ground, along with some old clothes. Christian's old armor was exposed, hanging perfectly off a metal outfit form.

"Wow," Adam accidentally said out loud, admiring the beauty and flawless lighting.

Christian took a breath as he saw the equipment that consumed his life for so long. He reviewed the scratches, burns, and marks on it, remembering how each of them was created during his prior battles. While it was nice to see the armor again for nostalgic purposes, he didn't feel an urge to put it back on again. Ever. In his mind, it would be no different than a drug addict in recovery returning to their habit. It would result in him losing his life one way or another.

Adam continued to stare and touched it, which was something he was never allowed to do, even when Christian was actively using it each night. "Hey, I know this is a weird question, but can I try it on?"

Christian stayed quiet but couldn't ignore the glow in his son's eyes, so he agreed. He helped Adam put it on, piece by piece, explaining the weapons and construction of each part.

Rebecca heard the strange noises and went downstairs to see what her boys were doing. As she completed the final step down, Christian stood before Adam, both of them seeing him in full armor for the first time. It was a little big for his body size but mostly fit. Her chest immediately tightened, and her anxiety ramped up. Aside from seeing Caroline's little body at the service they had held in her hospital room after she was murdered, this was the next worst thing she could imagine seeing.

"Oh my," she said out loud, putting her hand across her chest.

"Oh, hi, Mom," Adam said, looking at himself in a mirror and admiring the sight.

"Honey, we just put it on for fun. It's going back right now," Christian told her in a bit of a panic.

Rebecca had flashbacks of sitting with her husband as he was bleeding, burned, and mauled after run-ins with Blackheart. And the pairing of those memories coupled with the sight of

Adam would be a bit too much for any mother to withstand. She politely smiled and went back upstairs to remove herself from the situation before she reprimanded both.

"Shit, looks like we're both in trouble, kiddo," Christian joked. "But you look awesome."

They smiled at one another and hugged briefly. They worked as a team, putting the armor back into its designated space among the clutter. Adam went upstairs, not sure whether his mother would yell at him. Christian remained downstairs. He started to toss the tarp back over the armor but continued looking at his old gear. The suit had something significant left to do in his life. Just as he knew all those years that Blackheart would return, it was just a feeling he had. He hoped it didn't involve him putting the armor back on for some dire reason. Each time he used to wear it, he felt it would be his last night alive. He loosely covered the armor with the small tarp and followed Adam upstairs.

14

Evil Incarnate

Months later, the construction was completed on Chrysanthemum Drive. Blackheart still grimaced in the hidden underground cellar, listening to the noise from above.

He communicated with a now fully awakened John Smith, commanding him to rise up and regain control of his town. Smith had managed to slowly crawl through the loose, fresh soil, nearing the surface. As the one small tractor was moved off the area, Smith was able to free himself and stood on his own power. The large machinery blocked him from the sunlight.

The sun was setting, but the low level of light displayed the ghastly figure. Smith was covered in dirt, with ghostly white, sickly, paper-thin patches of skin, and he had absolutely no hair on any part of his body. His facial features were exaggerated due to the protuberances from his skull. He had no nose, and his eyes were sunken into his head. His elongated fingers and toes looked like talons. There were various cracks and holes throughout his body that housed many types of worms, spiders, and insects that came with him from the ground. They all walked around inside and on top of him at their leisure like loyal pets. Most of his clothes had deteriorated during his slumber, but a few shreds of black cloth remained hanging.

Smith looked around and wiggled his arms and legs, sending some of the spiders dangling from webs. They quickly crawled back into him. He snapped his teeth a few times, repositioning his jaw, feeling weakened but still strong enough to feed.

He moved slowly, approaching one of the stocky construction workers and quickly bit his throat with large canines. He drank the blood, which was nowhere near as potent as Blackheart's but enough to satisfy Smith. His energy increased, but it did not result in any physical alterations. Unknowingly, he was far too old and decomposed to look like his former self. The most benefit he would yield from feeding was an increase in energy and a tiny bit of strength. Since vampires stuck to their own territories and it was extremely rare that they returned from the dead, this portion of their mythology was not well-known among the creatures. He knew only that the blood in the soil kept him in suspended unconsciousness for a long time, and something else took the long lasting energy left in his body, rejuvenating it.

Smith continued to walk around, observing his freshly built and pristine home. He smiled so wide that the right side of his mouth split up his cheek. He casually walked around the entire property, biting every one of the workers one by one. He didn't kill them but rather let them all live so they would be submissive and serve him. Each of them turned into a unique and horrific type of vampire within mere minutes of being attacked. Some grew long, pale faces with lizard-like eyes, others saw their ears lengthen and teeth grow to the point of sticking out of their mouths like swords, and some even retained their human appearances but had enormous canines. The entire group became an eclectic mix of the undead.

Smith heard the thoughts Blackheart placed into his mind but wasn't aware of the origin. Smith knew only that he was alive and would regain his town once again with the help of his minions. He also had a feeling that his former victim, Timothy, was still alive somewhere, and he wanted to get a mouthful of the sweetest blood he ever tasted. No dirt would convolute the flavor. He wanted it in the purest form, directly from his most favorite child victim. The one child he took everything from, except his essence. All that would now change.

15

Odd Discovery

L ate that same night, Christian's police squad performed another safety check on Chrysanthemum Drive. There was nobody on-site, and all the unit found were various signs of struggle and blood, in addition to the hole in the ground. The unit quickly drew their weapons, with half of the officers checking the woods around the area and the others inside the house. Nothing was found.

"Christian, you need to get out here. Something's terribly wrong," the officer communicated over his radio.

Christian knew his fears were becoming a reality. Without hesitation, he ran out of the police station and jumped into a patrol car. He sped to Chrysanthemum Drive, fearing for the safety of his officers. He arrived to see all his men visibly uneasy. He paced around the property and noticed at least a dozen pairs of footprints leading into the woods but then disappearing. Unsure of what had happened, he resisted the urge to pursue.

Come on, Christian. Last year, you would've walked into those woods with no one at your back. Look at you now. You've lost your edge, his inner voice barked at him.

He turned away from the woods and walked toward the deep hole in the ground. Along the way, he saw a few spurts of blood along the equipment, but there were no bodies anywhere.

"What happened, Mr. Reed?" one of the officers called out.

He ignored the question and removed his flashlight to peer down into the hole. He saw little bits of bone and worn skin that resembled aged leather. Along the side of the hole were deep claw marks. Smith's body hadn't been buried deep enough to avoid being disrupted by the construction. He was back, somehow, and had others following him now.

"Is this Blackheart again? Is he back?" another officer called.

"Smith," Christian muttered to himself, fully realizing what had happened. "John Smith is back."

Christian ran back to his squad car and called the police chief.

"Chief, we have a problem out here on Chrysanthemum Drive. John Smith is back."

"What?" The chief yelled into his phone. "Jesus Christ, I'll get the other officers off the road and out to you ASAP. I'm getting my shoes on now to come out too."

Christian then put through a similar call with Wiggins, who mostly stayed quiet on the call, glad to hear the police chief responded with alarm.

"What have we done?" Wiggins kept repeating during the conversation.

Christian hung up his phone and went back out to address his officers again. "Guys, I want you all to go get your riot gear from HQ. You're all about to get a big lesson on why this division exists. Call your wives, girlfriends, and whoever else too. We're all being held over indefinitely."

They all looked at one another and followed orders. Even though some of men were scared, they were all loyal to Christian and felt some degree of comfort that he was the best person to depend on during a crisis like this.

Christian remained behind and quickly called Alexandra, who informed him of her recent dream. Both knew none of this was a coincidence. Meadowsville was in immediate danger.

Christian told her to remain in place until he let her know otherwise and then called his wife to do the same with Adam. The feelings of excitement and fright were things he had relished not too long ago. But now, he was deathly afraid of a threat that he couldn't even imagine in his worst nightmares.

* * *

As Christian hung up his phone, Blackheart's large, gnarled nostrils sniffed the air from the cold, dark cellar, and he recognized his once great opponent. He smiled to himself and knew his plan was coming together. He would be back sooner than he had hoped. And he took solace, knowing that when he eventually returned to see Christian, the man would be no more worrisome than an ant.

And who could forget sweet Alexandra. With her over-confidence and lovely face. This vibrant young woman, who Blackheart also depended on at one point, was now unnecessary. *I wish I could have tasted her blood one more time.* He quickly pulled himself out of the fantasy, knowing he no longer had a need for blood or either of those people. He would now just have to relish watching their terrified faces as he rained down a degree of destruction never before imagined in this world. His entertainment was the only purpose they now served.

16

Group Feeding

Later that same day, former Department of Public Works parks and grounds supervisor Johnny Mays, now working for the Meadowsville Electric Company, was preparing to climb down the newly repaired cell tower that had been damaged by Blackheart. It took several months for them to restore power and functionality, but it was now done and ready. Luckily, this was only one of the many towers across Meadowsville.

After some downsizing at the public works department over the last year, Mays had to return to his original technical training to make ends meet. He missed his prior job because it paid more and was much less labor intensive.

"All this stupid shit and I'm stuck up here. Vampires and all this garbage," he muttered.

Mays looked out at the dusk sky and began packing up his tools. He wiped his forehead with his arm, leaving a trail of grease along his nose. He carefully put his tools over his right shoulder and shimmied to the ladder to descend. As he placed his foot down onto the first rung, several large spiders crawled out of his sleeve and onto his hands. They were varied colors, all moving in separate directions. He swatted at them and lost his footing, slipping, but fortunately got a tight grip on the rusted metal ladder.

Mays shrugged off the arachnids that now seemed to stay a few feet overhead, watching him. He caught his breath after the scary experience and climbed down a few more rungs but then noticed several more spiders crawling up.

Then someone spoke to him from below. "Hold on tight. I want you tight. Tight makes it feel better."

He looked down at the distant voice and saw John Smith muttering foul things up at him, not knowing who or what this phantom was. Branching up from the creature was a trail of thousands of bugs and insects crawling toward him. Surrounding Smith were a dozen grotesque-looking monsters staring up at him with hungry eyes. Drool dripped or poured out of each of their mouths. He was in serious trouble.

Mays tried to climb back up but his hands and feet squashed the bugs around the ladder. Their innards and blood caused him to slide down, despite his best efforts. He caught himself again on a small portion of a dry rung, trying desperately to hurry away from his tormentors.

Smith raised his boney arm and pointed up at him. His group of vampires effortlessly climbed the tower on all sides. Some crawled up, resembling the bugs, while other leaped.

Mays was terrified and realized he stood no chance against the creatures. Struggling to escape, he threw his tool bag down at them but was caught within seconds. They scooped him up while he yelled and screamed for help. As the vampires reached and then overpowered him, they pulled him toward the top of the tower and impaled him at the crest.

Mays did not perish quickly but felt pain through his abdomen and the blood leaving his body. His last sight was the darkening sky above. His blood poured down the tower in multiple fine trails as each of the monsters licked their own personal drip.

Smith looked up at the attack and smirked with his almost fully disintegrated mouth.

As each of the vampires gracefully descended the tower, they lined up single file in front of Smith and tilted their heads down. Smith looked at his posse and slowly went to each of them, sampling their blood, going from oldest at the front to youngest at the back. Smith always preferred the taste of younger blood. He took notice of a flyer blowing across the pavement below, advertising the *Peter Pan* play at the East Meadowsville Elementary that night.

17

Broadcasted Chaos

A male news anchor interrupted the normal broadcast. "We have breaking news from the Channel 1 newsroom. We've gotten several reports of the sudden disappearance of a dozen workers at the very controversial reconstruction on Chrysanthemum Drive. Let's go on scene with Jacob J. Jenson."

The broadcast shifted to a chaotic scene at the mansion site. Christian and his men were seen trying to push the media off the grounds, securing it with police barriers and tape, while they continued to investigate. Christian reluctantly agreed to a few questions in exchange for the press to back away from the scene.

"Please, please, I'm from Channel 1 news. Can you tell us what happened?"

"I can't comment on an ongoing investigation. But I assure you all that we're working as quickly as possible."

The cameraman cut to the gaping hole in the ground and a few bloody handprints on the remaining tractors. One of Christian's officers tried to forcefully redirect the one camera to avoid the footage but was unsuccessful.

"That looks like blood. Is this from vandals, or do you think Mr. Smith is back? Or Blackheart?"

Christian shoved Jenson to the ground as he lost his patience. "Don't start with that kinda talk. You're trying to scare people for ratings. We don't know what happened yet. And it's shit like this that causes residents to panic over nothing."

Jenson cut off his exchange with Christian, turning his head and listening to his earpiece as his station manager told him about the murder at the phone tower.

He looked back at Christian and stopped brushing the dirt off his suit with a grin. "Mr. Reed, we're just being told that there is a murder atop the central cell tower. That would be incident two today. Are we still causing people to panic over nothing? And why is your squad on scene and not the regular police?"

Christian started sweating as his anxiety ramped up from his instinctual feeling that there was an evil presence in town again. "I can't comment on that," he said, unsure what to do.

The newsfeed cut to the cell tower, where other police officers were looking up and attempting to retrieve the slaughtered body of Johnny Mays. They were seen struggling against the green ooze leftover by the bugs, and they were unable to get to the body. One officer called for a ladder truck from the fire department. Several other officers in riot gear pushed the media coverage back toward the road, as far away from the scene as they could manage.

Another sharply dressed reporter took over the newscast, briefly managing to get beyond the police barriers. "Thanks, Darrel. This is Brody Banner reporting from on location. As you can see, there are grisly scenes from the eastern portion of Meadowsville. In addition to the missing workers from Chrysanthemum Drive, we now have a confirmed fatality. It does not look like a suicide but rather a homicide. Christian Reed's MPS also being on scene at Chrysanthemum Drive indicates that Meadowsville may be dealing with yet another preternatural issue. Just our luck."

Brody and his cameraman were finally removed from their position by one of the police officers. As he was being dragged away, the cameraman zoomed in on the impaled body and the dried blood all over the top of the tower.

"Are the rumors true? Is it Mr. Smith? Blackheart? Something else? The people of this town have been through enough. They deserve to know what's happening," one of the other reporters called out to the police.

None of the police responded to the questions, but they kept the media at bay.

* * *

Mayor Wiggins sat in his office, watching the broadcast, and then started crying. He made it a point to not to hide in his office, but with the stress of everything going on lately, he'd resorted to it. Fewer people had access to him this way, and he could hide for however long he needed to on a given day.

He spoke with Christian earlier about his investigation on Chrysanthemum Drive, and they agreed something was happening. If only he had listened to his gut instinct and fought against the memorial site being created, this would have been avoided.

"I can't believe this is happening again. I failed them. I don't deserve to be here anymore," he said to himself, feeling a world of guilt.

He again thought of his loving wife, Eleanor, and his projected image of her disappointed face.

Christian called the mayor's office again, but Wiggins didn't hear it over his sobbing.

18

Play Time

Christian and Mayor Wiggins sat across from each other in his office that night. Wiggins's face was red at the cheeks and around his eyes; it was clear he had cried very recently. Christian was sweaty, stressed, and anxious. Neither man felt ready for the conversation that needed to happen.

"So, you think John Smith is doing this?" Wiggins asked Christian.

"I believe so. But we don't have evidence of anything except for the body of the technician, so it's hard to say. The construction workers are all missing. So we have only one confirmed fatality and nothing else."

"What the hell is happening out there?" Wiggins asked, standing up and looking out at the town, crossing his hands behind his back.

"I don't know. I don't know how a lot of this works. None of us do. There may be people out in the world with more experience, but who knows? That hole right next to the mansion and the murder and disappearances—it has to be Smith. Literally no other explanation."

"Couldn't be Blackheart again, right?"

"God, I hope not. Seems very doubtful though."

"Okay, so let's assume it is Smith. The police have been checking the woods around the property all day, and there're no tracks, dead animals, or anything. How did you guys find nothing out there?"

"I don't know, but we're on it."

"I hope so. I really do. I was the most prominent person behind this MPS experiment. This is the time that you guys need to show your worth so everyone else sees your value too."

Christian nodded.

"Now, what about Smith? How do we even find him?"

"Simple. Follow the children, and he won't be far behind. He was a vicious pedophile, so he's going to regain enough strength and then go after the children of this town again." Christian had a sudden realization. "And based off the old stories, he only hunted at night. We know that much."

Mayor Wiggins paled at Christian's words, remembering the dozens of children being pulled out of the cellar on Chrysanthemum Drive last year, all crying for their parents. He then noticed Christian focusing on a paper hanging off one of Wiggins's corkboards. It was a flyer for the play tonight.

"What's wrong?"

"There is a play tonight at Rebecca's elementary school. The flyers are everywhere. He had to have seen it. That's Smith's next target," Christian said, darting out of the office.

He quickly phoned the police chief while getting into the cruiser. He brought all his men back on duty, just as most of them were being relieved for a few hours to rest.

Unfortunately, rest would have to wait. He ordered them to suit up and get to East Meadowsville Elementary; he was highly suspicious of Mr. Smith attending it. Even if he were wrong, which he doubted, he would rather play things safe than be sorry.

* * *

Meanwhile, at the elementary school, Rebecca Reed stood in the back of the audience as the children in her third-grade class reenacted *Peter Pan*. One student, who had on an adorable crocodile suit, circled a makeshift cardboard pirate ship that gently tilted back and forth. Another student, dressed as Peter Pan, was hanging from a secured safety harness, circling overhead around a student below playing Captain Hook. They demonstrated a most intense battle with Styrofoam swords. The room darkened, and Rebecca smiled at her students' hard work on this play.

"Roar!" the crocodile yelled in a high-pitched voice.

The parents in attendance chuckled at the adorable display, and there was a sincere, warm feeling in the room.

The entrance doors next to Rebecca opened, and she assumed a parent was coming late. But the doors weren't opened gently. They were pulled back with force. She turned to see who was entering but could only hear heavy breathing and muffled moaning. John Smith took a single step in, far enough for her to see his ghoulish appearance. He didn't acknowledge her at all but just stared eagerly at the children. A half-rotted tongue stuck out of his now completely lipless face and massaged the corner of his mouth that was split at the skin. Several worms crawled out of missing pieces of his cheek and then into other openings in his scalp. Rebecca wanted to scream but couldn't believe her eyes; she was frozen in place.

"Hmm . . . I love it when they're in little costumes. Easy to take off with their skin still attached," he mumbled to himself, making a soft fist with both hands.

Coming out of her shock, Rebecca crept away from Smith, trying not to alert the other parents yet. Smith began to rub his thighs, with thin layers of skin peeling off and landing on the ground like dirty feathers. Rebecca noticed Smith's other creatures directly outside the entranceway, waiting for their leader to give direction. Without further hesitation, she pulled the fire alarm and shoved Smith out the doors into his followers, locking them all out. The audience all jumped up and scattered in a frenzy as she blocked them from the door that was keeping Smith out.

"The fire is out there. Grab your children and go through the emergency exit," she yelled, struggling to hold the doors as the vampires tried to force them open.

After a minute, the doors were pulled off their hinges. Rebecca saw the group and feared for her life but worried more about everyone else. Even if they made quick work of her, she was willing to sacrifice herself to give all her students and their loved ones a few seconds advantage to escape. Smith seemed to float toward her and opened his mouth, sticking out his last two remaining teeth, which looked like two daggers. She felt, and now fully appreciated, the hatred her husband felt for Blackheart. As Rebecca readied herself to fight back, a gunshot rang out suddenly, catching everyone's attention. She looked beyond the vampires and saw Christian and a dozen of his squad members, in protective gear with their weapons drawn.

"Over here, you ugly bastards," Christian yelled, leading his men into battle against the pack of monsters.

Smith walked away from Rebecca, who ran in the opposite direction. He pushed past his followers and allowed Christian to see the legend in person for the first time.

Christian was not afraid. His anger outweighed his fear as seeing his wife in danger drove his emotions into a state of disarray. He smiled at his wife, who did the same to him, and she ran to make sure all of her guests and students were safe.

"There you are," Christian said to himself, trying to look into Smith's eyes, which were sunk deep into his skull.

Smith growled at Christian and waved his hand, signaling the vampires to attack. He slowly walked down the walkway toward the stage, sniffing like a hungry dog along the way. He could smell the fresh scent of the children and remembered just how much he loved it. The harness hung over the stage, making a slight squeaking noise as it swayed. A drop of sweat, from the student playing Peter Pan, was left on the stage. Smith crawled onto the elevated surface and licked it, taking a moment to appreciate the taste. Afterward, he casually walked back into the hallway, watching the battle ensue. He walked past the action, unharmed and unafraid of it all, in a saunter.

The officers fired accurately at the vampires that danced around them, crawling across the walls and ceiling, shrieking at the tops of their lungs. Christian grabbed one of them by the hair and put a silver bullet in its head, leaving it in a lifeless form. He wondered why these vampires died so easily, compared to Blackheart. He then realized his nemesis was more than what these monstrosities were, and he might very well be an active part of this attack from Smith.

Christian felt the pain from his old injuries but was able to push through. He couldn't fight like he used to, and he needed to work as a team with his squad. If not, they were all at risk of getting killed.

Another vampire grabbed Christian and slammed him against a fire hydrant, attempting to bite him. Officer Cyders put the monster in a choke hold and stabbed it in the eye with a silver knife; he pulled the blade down through its shoulder, killing it. Christian remembered using a similar maneuver to kill one of Blackheart's hounds all those years ago. Cyders helped Christian up, and they gave each other a look of understanding and respect. The young officer fully acknowledged his prior skepticism and disrespect of his squad's leader, and he was remorseful.

The two sides battled as Christian's unit saw four officers heavily injured, but they were able to push the rest of Smith's wounded group out of the opposite end of the school, saving every attendee and student from harm.

All but two of the vampires disappeared into the night like shadows, and Smith slowly walked behind them, alone and unafraid. Christian watched him in disbelief, helping to give first aid measures to his wounded men before the first responders arrived.

Smith watched Christian, having no idea who this man was. But he knew the man had encountered vampires before. Before walking out the school doors, Smith turned and locked eyes with Christian, who could now see what was left of the recessed brown eyes; Smith smiled like they were the best of friends. Christian sneered, watching Smith leave the grounds and go into the woods with his clan. He then looked at the pair of dead vampires on the tiled floor of the school, realizing he had a head wound.

Shortly after, more members of the MPD arrived alongside several ambulances. They checked out the students and parents outside, who were all filled with fear after the attempted massacre. Christian was in tears, watching a few of his men get taken away in ambulances. One died from blood loss, in his arms, before the EMTs were able to arrive. Christian sat, praying for the officer as he stayed with him, holding his hand, helping him calmly transition into death. The last time he held a dead body was his daughter, Caroline. It was horrible to do sixteen long years ago, and today was no different.

Rebecca found him among the chaos. She saw him near tears and covered in blood. This was unfortunately a sight that she had become accustomed to, with his many years of acting as a lone vigilante. But he looked more human now. And she was glad to see it. She ran to him, hugging and kissing him passionately. Christian let himself cry, feeling secure in Rebecca's embrace.

"I'm so glad you're okay," she said.

"I thought they were going to get you. Just like Caroline," he said, hugging her hard.

"They didn't. I'm here."

"Thank you for being here," he said, putting his forehead to hers.

"We saved everyone."

"I lost a man," he cried, not looking up at her, burying his face in the side of her neck. "I failed them."

"Honey, you did your best," she said, holding his by the face gently. "You did your best."

Christian was inconsolable, even with her reassurances. They hugged again, just happy that they were both still alive.

"Blackheart is back. It's got to be him," one of the worried parents yelled out.

Christian wiped his tears and looked far away, into the woods across from the elementary school. He saw several pairs of the vampires' eyes glowing from the flashing lights of all the first responder's vehicles. They stayed in place, enjoying the chaos.

* * *

Blackheart sat in the cellar, feeling satisfaction as his name was becoming relevant once again. His already immense power was slowly increasing. As Smith continued to bring fear to the residents, Blackheart would eventually be able to return and bring vengeance to the world.

His world.

"Enjoying this?" he asked God, who remained silent at the taunt.

19

New Plan

An emergency council meeting was held early the next morning, with a large number of residents attending. The group yelled at Mayor Wiggins, who stood idly at the podium where he once had felt comfortable speaking. He seemed much more detached than he had in recent memory. He appeared unshaven, unkempt, and unfocused and had dark circles under his eyes from not sleeping. Before he had stepped to the podium, the council members informed him they were out of options. He was sickened by what had to be passed on the agenda. The damning declarations of each of the members rattled in his brain.

"Wiggins, we're tired of waiting around and letting your ideas not *work. This town is up shit's creek because of your leadership, and if you don't commit to this, we will make sure you*

aren't reelected in November. We are all in agreement that this is the only option left."

"Agreed. The MPS and everything else has been a public disaster."

"You're failing and letting everyone down. You are a liar and bring shame to these people."

"Either you're with us or we'll find a candidate that is. He needs to be brought back. End of story."

"Okay, everyone, shut up," Wiggins called out in anger, silencing the room. "I can't listen to this anymore. This can't continue. This town is falling apart, and I'm sick of it. People are scared, and we have at least two deaths on our hands now. We will not allow ourselves to be prey for these creatures any longer. This town will not be victimized again!"

The crowd erupted at his powerful proclamation. Christian sat quietly behind the mayor, among the council members and department heads, exhausted and upset. Alexandra sat near the front with Adam and Rebecca, worried for her friend and ally. She attempted to speak with some of the other church leaders before the meeting started, but they just walked away from her. Her efforts were fruitless. The anger in the room felt like it did when Blackheart was still running the town. The goodwill and faith was dissipating at an alarming rate, and there was nothing she could do.

"We thought your unit could prevent this. Or even handle it, God forbid it happened," one of the councilman spoke out to Christian.

"I thought so too. I'm sorry we didn't do more," Christian responded, still too distraught to say much else.

"At least your wife saved everyone in the school. You lost one man, and we have four others on the shelf," a police officer called out.

Christian's anger boiled over. "Hey, fuck you. I'd like to see your fat fuckin' ass out there risking your life for this town like we do each and every night. You should be thanking us for controlling that scene last night. If we weren't there, that whole building would've been a graveyard. And how dare you use my wife to get under my skin. You should be thanking her, not disrespecting our family."

"People are dead. Your job is to prevent this kind of thing," another council member called out.

"We did our best. This isn't like it was before," Christian defended himself.

"Can Festiville or Veronia give us additional police coverage?" Councilman Miller asked the mayor.

"No, everyone is scared and unwilling to help. And they've got their own issues going on," Wiggins responded. "And the surrounding towns still treat us like outcasts. This is all being looked at like a scheme to make money. None of them believe in Smith or Blackheart or any of it. They've begun closing off the city lines in our direction. It looks like we're on our own."

"They don't believe in the pictures, dead bodies, or any of it?"

"From my brief conversations with their administrations, they believe it's all doctored documents and pictures. None of it genuine. You can thank Mayor Wilkins, God rest her soul, for them feeling this way. She was the worst offender out of any of the past administrations."

The crowd groused, and the mayor looked at Christian. Wiggins's guilt for what he was about to present grew alongside Christian's hostility.

"I am willing to do whatever it takes to protect us," Wiggins told the room. "Even going to extreme measures."

The residents all sat, unsure of what he referred to.

Wiggins swallowed hard and prepared to make a very risky statement. "I think we're at a point where we need to look at other options. Things that we may not like but may have to yield to."

The audience quieted themselves completely.

Wiggins looked directly at Alexandra, who was praying quietly. He felt sick to his stomach that he was about to betray both Christian and Alexandra, because both were responsible for giving significant contributions to the town, saving it from near destruction on more than one occasion.

"Alexandra," he called out.

She looked up with her mesmerizing green eyes.

"We all know the stories now. You both resurrected and killed Blackheart. You were the one who put him to rest once and for all. And you did it with nonviolent means. It was with your faith that both miracles were performed."

She nodded slowly.

"I think if there is a way to bring him back, we should entertain the thought."

The crowd started yelling again, denouncing the very thought of it.

Blackheart sat in his current dwelling, feeling a sudden surge of power from their mention of him in a large group of the residents.

"First off, I think that's a dangerous and horrid suggestion. Second, it can't be done. Third, even if it could, I wouldn't be a part of it," Alex responded, sickened by the proposal.

Some of the audience members who had lost loved ones to the town's troubled past also voiced their displeasure at the thought. The council sat in silence behind the mayor, which Alexandra took notice of.

"Oh, I see. This is something you've all discussed before this meeting," Alex prodded.

Christian stood up in a rage.

"We have no other options left," Wiggins said.

"You're playing with fire. This is ridiculous. Do you all have a death wish? How many times are you going to subject yourselves to this evil?" Christian said loudly, hoping more of Meadowsville supported his feelings.

The mayor slightly turned to the council, and two of the members nodded at him to continue as they had discussed prior to this town hall assembly.

"Then, Christian, I'm sorry to announce that due to the unanimous vote of the council, after the recent events, your squad is suspended. Your officers will be put on regular patrol duty and you are being put on leave until internal affairs investigates everything that's happened with the MPS."

"What?" Christian yelled back.

"It is the decision of this council," Wiggins proclaimed.

"I can't believe this," Christian said in protest. "You guys haven't learned. You'll never learn. Just like before. You're going to have tens of thousands of deaths on your heads. I've done my part. I'm done." He stood up, kicking and breaking his chair. "Take that out of my paycheck, while you're at it."

"Christian, this wasn't an easy decision. We cannot risk any more lives being lost. Your unit and the PD cannot maintain order, the surrounding towns have isolated us and refuse to help, and we are in dire need of assistance. We know we can kill Blackheart. We've done it before with both the help of yourself and Miss Hughes. As my grandfather used to say, 'Sometimes, you have to burn the village to win the war.'"

"I won't be involved. Neither of us will," Alexandra said of her and Christian. "What you're suggesting is insane. You have no idea what kind of elements you're toying with. This is on a biblical scale. It is so much bigger than you realize. My father knew that, and so do I now. And it needs to be respected and left alone. We were lucky enough to escape it twice, but to willingly let it happen again? There's no excuse for it. There have to be other ways to deal with Smith."

"How? Arm the citizens and ask them to form their own militias? Just like all those years ago? How well did that work out?" Wiggins replied.

The audience all shook their heads, trying to wrap their minds around the discussion.

"Mayor Wiggins, I highly respect you. But this is not the way to do things. I know this is an election year, but you can't let this council sway you on a knee-jerk reaction like this."

"Alexandra, I am ordering you and the other church leaders to develop a plan to resurrect Blackheart. End of discussion," Wiggins cut her off, angry at her questioning of his intentions.

Alex stood in thought for a few seconds before beginning to walk toward the exit; Christian joined her. No one in the crowd followed them, and after further discussion, everyone seemed to agree with the administration.

"I'm sorry to see that. Alexandra, your funding from the town is now cut too."

She stopped, tempted to keep fighting, but decided to ignore the condemnation of the mayor and council. Adam and Rebecca both left the meeting, too, visibly unnerved.

"God help us," Alexandra called out. "You'll be in my prayers. And, boy, are you going to need them."

As Alex and Christian stormed out, the other church leaders agreed to develop a plan to resurrect Blackheart without Alexandra's involvement. The audience unanimously voted in favor of the motion. Some of them did so solely to further upset Alexandra, while the others agreed with Wiggins that the killings needed to stop.

Blackheart felt another surge and punched the ceiling of the cellar, cracking it. This delighted him immensely. He looked at what used to be hands but now resembled claws; he admired his new appearance, along with the powers he kept with him when he was sent back to earth. His time was near.

Christian brought Alexandra outside and detailed a plan he'd developed last year to prevent the resurrection of any more potential vampires. "I believe they can only be brought back when their bodies are intact and exposed to the blood of another vampire." He surmised that Smith and Blackheart's blood in the soil on Chrysanthemum Drive was the unknown dynamic that kept them both viable over the years.

He brought Alex to his squad office to empty out his desk at the police department and showed her a map and the names of every buried victim. They would have to act quickly, as there were hundreds of bodies.

In case he was wrongfully terminated, Christian also gave instructions to his remaining officers. "I want you to begin secretly digging the bodies up so they can be burned and not be at risk for coming back." His officers were few in number but still loyal to his cause.

Alexandra offered her help to them, knowing David's body would need to be addressed. They would have to act at night, and quickly, as to not alert the other houses of worship of their intentions. The Meadowsville Community Church would be the first stop, as Christian put Alexandra's safety at the forefront.

20

Amplified Faith

Alexandra stood at her altar the next evening, seeing almost half of her congregation not present. Her refusal to partake in the Blackheart ceremony was something that took what was left of the dwindling faith of the community and split it divisively. She understood the power and influence she was saddled with after defeating Blackheart a year ago.

She preached but could not take her mind off the thought of seeing David once again. If they were successful in bringing back Blackheart, could the same be done to David? What if somehow he was brought back but wasn't in his right mind? Would she be able to lose him again? Or, God forbid, have to kill him herself? The mere concept of reopening that long-standing wound on her emotions mirrored the injury she had dealt to Blackheart. She'd seen the gash reopen on the creature last year, and that was what her heart would do upon seeing David again.

While she spent many years doubting her own strength and integrity, the traumatic events she had been part of had made her stronger, more confident, and spiritually ready to do what she felt was best. She just had to stay the course and trust in herself, which was what her father, Father Richard, had continually instilled in her. And as she matured and had more experiences, both in and out the church, his advice had continued to be on point.

While not pleasant in the current moment, she stared at her audience and realized they needed her to be strong. Not just for herself but for them. She, and the other church leaders in town, were the facilitators for these people to find and have their own unique relationships with God. They had had many months to respond to her pleas for the greater good, but most ignored them out of spite for her abilities and the free will of the people.

She became sterner as she preached but reassured herself she was doing everything the way it needed to be done. She had been in training for the current situation and would rise to the task at hand, no matter what. If this was indeed the ultimate test of faith for Meadowsville, she would lead the fight and help bring them to ultimate and permanent salvation. She then paused, looking out toward the cemetery, where Christian's police unit was digging up specific grave sites to burn.

21

Bigger Picture

Ⓣhis is Gabriel Connors from Channel 1 News. We are here with several members of the Meadowsville religious community. With the recent decision to attempt to resurrect Blackheart, the town is heavily divided. The surrounding areas are also very concerned, even going as far as to have police blockades at their town lines. So, let's open this up. Thank you all for coming today."

Ten diverse church leaders sat on camera, recorded from in their respective offices, and thanked the anchor for having them on.

"So, in case you've lived under a rock, Blackheart is a controversial figure. A being of unknown supernatural abilities. He killed potentially thousands of citizens in Meadowsville over several decades. With the help of local citizens, Christian Reed and Alexandra Hughes teamed up to defeat the monster on two separate occasions. Now the town and its administration have voted to bring back this thing to battle a previous but similar problem in John Smith, aka Mr. Smith. What say you?"

"It's willingly opening ourselves up to hell on earth. We are asking that the devil be brought back to save us. Because we aren't willing to allow God to see things through," one pastor said.

"But God gives us all common sense. And with no other options left, this is what we have to do. Could you live with more lives lost?" a priest responded.

"This is how Revelations begins. The monsters are sent as the people are judged by the Antichrist. Blackheart is that figure."

"We must keep our faith during times like this. He will show us the way," another pastor called out.

"Even if he is brought back, God will keep him in line," another father spoke out.

"And if He doesn't? Can we be sure of that? We don't know what Blackheart's true intention will be. Is it to rule over Meadowsville? Or the world? We have absolutely no idea. It could be cataclysmic," a rabbi debated.

"The day God leaves us to ourselves is when we encounter the end of days. Doomsday. The apocalypse. It has so many terms. But if that happens, Meadowsville will be the end of us and the beginning of the end for mankind," another priest added in.

The debate continued for another fifteen minutes before Gabriel Connors cut them off and ended the discussion.

Blackheart felt more power come to him and punched his previous mark in the cellar, creating a spider web of cracks around it in the ceiling. He was almost there.

22

Modern History

L ater the next evening, Bruce and Adam sat in the Meadowsville Public Library piecing together their history project. They had been working for months on the project, almost living in the library when not in school. They were scanning every available piece of history from Meadowsville, both in electronic and hard-copy form. The head librarian, Mrs. Anderson, laughed to herself at how hard the boys were working. She had helped them find some of the information as they explained the depth of their assignment to her. The material was very broken up, and none of them could accurately determine what was truthful.

"Boys, remember, it only has to be ten pages. Don't kill yourselves over it," she called from the reference desk.

Bruce and Adam looked up and her and smiled at the joke before returning to their work. They managed to determine the start of the town's issues with John Smith abducting children; then Blackheart becoming one of his victims, taking over after Smith died. But going back to before the documented John Smith killings yielded very inadequate documentation.

"So once the Smiths, Martins, Fitzpatricks, and Bensons founded the town, there isn't really anything beyond that. Then the next piece of documentation suddenly shows the Smith lineage, which seems to be the only surviving family after the first few years," Adam said.

"Yeah, it just says the other families died of unknown causes. But close together. So how did Smith survive?"

"I wonder if the Smith family have always been vampires and ended up killing the others."

"Or they were all vampires and went to war with each other," Bruce suggested.

"Then why would they have all come here at the same time and lived among each other for so long?"

"Maybe there wasn't enough food for all of them, and it became a territory battle for survival. Like, they thought there would be, but there wasn't. So their clique went awry?"

"The Smith family had a lot of children. But they died young too."

"Maybe they weren't his kids. Maybe they were victims from nearby towns that he kept as slaves. That would explain the fear of Meadowsville early on. And the Smith family could use them to feed on while the other families struggled to survive."

Both boys sat looking at the books and thinking over the possibilities.

"And maybe that's why John Smith was the only vampire here all that time. And why he never left Meadowsville. He beat out all the others and kept this town as his trophy. He wouldn't let any more come in or leave," Adam said.

"Strong possibility," Bruce responded.

"Well, whatever we come up with, whether completely accurate or a little skewed, will be the start of some kind of paper trail on the town's history."

"It's really insane how much was covered up."

"So he always enjoyed the company of little kids. Really gross."

Bruce shut one of the books. A small group of beetles lay underneath it, scattering quickly onto the boys' laps. They brushed them off, and a myriad of other insects suddenly appeared around them.

Adam felt breath on the back of his neck. A small clump of his hair was then chewed off his head, making him quickly turn to be face-to-face with John Smith. He looked deep into the concave eye sockets, seeing nothing but blackness.

Smith stared Adam down, the hair falling out of his mouth as he grazed on it. Adam trembled as Bruce pulled him away, leading them both toward the one exit. They heard commotion from the librarian's office and saw Mrs. Anderson being pulled apart by several vampires. Adam and Bruce froze in fear at the scene they witnessed.

"You're John Smith, aren't you?" Adam asked.

Smith smiled, sending bugs out all across his face and onto his body. He took an engorged tick off his shoulder, popped it between his fingers, and licked the remains of the body off himself.

"This town was all mine one time. I had boys like you locked in my cellar all the time. The smell of your sweaty little armpits. The fear in your bodies gets me so hard. And the blood is so different. Like veal. Immature, but softer. More satisfying."

Smith looked at the books spread over the table. "I remember these people. I raped their children and ate their bodies. The history books won't ever show you that. I won this place fair and square. And died on my own terms."

Smith peered at Bruce then looked back at Adam.

"*Sooo* young but strong. I can still hold you down. Will you need to come up for air?" Smith muttered to both as he breathed deeper and loudly.

Smith took a worm out of a hole in his abdomen and ate it like a noodle as it crawled, unharmed, into another open area of his forehead. Adam and Bruce saw the other vampires finishing up their assault on Mrs. Anderson and quickly ran out the library exit. They retreated to Bruce's house a few blocks away. They both went inside and locked the door, exhausted from their sprint.

"I gotta call my dad," Adam said.

"That's probably a good idea. But, holy shit, who can say they got an in-person history lesson from John Smith and lived to tell the story?" Bruce joked.

Bruce found several weapons as they shut the lights off in the empty house, watching out the window to see whether John Smith followed them.

23

The Savior

That next morning, a perfect sunny day, several dozen church leaders and the local media surrounded the house on Chrysanthemum Drive. The house looked palatial, and the bright sky displayed its beauty. A slight odor from Lucerne Lake came through but was short-lived. The cameras took shots of the fresh white siding of the house, joined with black shutters, and the shine coming off the many brand-new windows.

All the attendees held hands, and the crowd fell silent under the instruction of the church leaders. They began a prayer they had developed together since the last town hall meeting, asking the residents to repeat after them:

"Lord, hear our prayers and feel our love for you. We have faith you will protect us from the evil that has returned to our town. We lay ourselves at your mercy and ask for help. We ask you to consider giving us this once troubled spirit one more time in its purest and most sincere form so he can fully repent his sins and serve you, as well as the town he hurt so much and for so long. We pray you will send him to us, as a reflection of yourself in an earthly form, so we can fully see your greatness and love for us, and so this town can rid ourselves of the evil spirits that linger here. Once and forever. Amen."

They all continued to hold hands and unify their efforts, feeding off the positive energy from one another. Blackheart felt stronger and abler as they prayed. He wanted them to want him back, thinking that he was God's symbol of hope and mercy. To serve him or die by his hand. He wanted to fool these people and destroy the entire town once and for all, making them all pay for enabling the pain he experienced there. Then he wanted to be done with Meadowsville and concentrate on his grander objective. With God having rejected him from heaven, he would rule over the world, becoming the only divinity they lived for. God would be forgotten, which would weaken him and strengthen Blackheart. And that would be the next step in his ultimate war against his almighty creator.

Blackheart backed up into the same corner that Smith abused him in so many times and charged the wall of the cement cellar, exploding through it with such force that it shook all of Meadowsville. Blackheart's strength was greater than he ever could have hoped. It made his tenure as a vampire seem irrelevant.

Both Alexandra and Christian felt it happen from the safety of their homes—both prayed against the return of Blackheart, but they knew what had happened.

He flew upward and high into the sky, flinging pieces of cement and dirt hundreds of feet into the air. All the attendees ran away to avoid being struck by debris but stopped at a secure distance, looking up at the hopeful figure in the sky.

The sunlight covered Blackheart. It now gave him energy and strength. It no longer weakened him, as it did years ago when he lived as a vampire. He stayed in the air, looking down at his previous home, now resembling a shrine to him. His large shadow symbolically covered the entire property and the people below. They looked up to him, all continuing to say their own prayers, thanking God for answering them.

He slowly and elegantly descended toward the ground. As his feet touched the surface, everyone got down on one knee, worshipping this supposed servant of God.

He saw his appearance in one of the windows of the mansion. He had snoutlike nose, multiple layers of razor-sharp, blackened fangs, scaly dark blue skin, and a long trail of pitch black hair that seemed to stand up like spikes down his entire back. The bones in his face and parts of his body were exaggerated, contorting him to look like a dragon-like hybrid. His body was bare, large and lean but still very muscular, resembling built-in armor. He had no clothes and no gender-specific anatomical features. His eyes were a smoldering deep orange, with two large bronze-colored horns sticking straight up out of the sides of his head.

"Our savior," he heard someone say. "Thank you, God!"

Blackheart could barely contain his excitement at finally getting the ultimate opportunity to challenge God on an entirely new level. He would take this world and all his people with him. God's supposed ultimate creations would be under Blackheart's rule now.

"As the Father has loved me, I promise to do the same unto you all," Blackheart commanded, spouting believable lies to the townspeople below.

They all cheered and hugged each other, not at all fearing Blackheart's extreme new appearance.

"Why have you summoned me back here? Ask, and it will be given to you."

"Blackheart . . . we need you to save us. John Smith is bringing upon us an evil that we cannot stop," a pastor called out. "You are our only hope."

Blackheart looked up at the sky, feeling the sun beat down on him, and embraced it. He smiled in victory, at God's expense, showing Meadowsville he would be their savior. He whistled so loud that it hurt the ears of his attendees, and a large flock of crows surrounded him, blocking the sun behind him so the audience could see his ultimate form. Much like his former hounds and vultures, he enjoyed having the companionship of animals around him. He instilled himself in them, forcing the creatures to see him as their leader, making them feel his raw power over them. It didn't matter to him whether he was worshipped by free will or fear.

"I will save you. All of you. All I ask is that you love me. Me and me alone. The same respect you give to the Lord. I am here, in His name and of His own image, for you. I am the Second Coming."

The people now went down on their knees, bowing to his decree and nonverbally agreeing to his request. He blessed and thanked them, flying into the sky at tremendous speed. Everyone jumped up, rejoicing, for their supposed savior was now here on earth.

24

Old Feelings

H e will wipe away every tear from their eyes, and death shall be no more, neither shall be mourning, nor crying, nor pain anymore, for the former things have passed away," Alexandra said as Christian set another body ablaze in its grave while some of his officers ran to another grave and started digging up another corpse. "How many more do we have?"

Christian pulled a list out of his pocket and made an ugly face at the remaining bodies that needed to be "treated." Despite the bodies being embalmed before being buried, they were taking no chances.

"Enough," he replied, watching the fire as his men extinguished it.

Alexandra looked down at the body that was now nothing more than a pile of dust with some random pieces of bone.

They continued through several more bodies in Alexandra's graveyard and reached David's location, which was now uncovered. David's body lay there, looking almost as he did the last time he was alive, aside from the wound across his neck that Blackheart had dealt him. Christian thought back to battling against and alongside David, back when Christian was much younger and abler.

Alexandra could not handle seeing him lying there lifeless, his soft brown hair, white skin, and full lips just as she remembered. Her final memory up to this point was when he kissed her shortly before going to die by Blackheart's hand. Alex and Christian stood there, not speaking or moving, as she started to tear up.

"What do we do?" Christian asked her.

"I dunno," she replied, heartbroken. "I tried to put him behind me, but it's like he and I have more to do together. Like there's something left that's keeping our connection so strong."

Christian softened. "He was a good kid. I know how much he meant to you." He paused. "But we have to keep working. Time is not on our side here."

"I know," Alex said, shedding more tears.

"I know this is hard for you. Would you rather I just do it?" he asked, trying to hand her matches and gasoline.

"No. Just not right now. I will. Just not now."

Christian nodded and continued to the next grave. Alex stayed behind with David and remembered how much she missed him. What she wouldn't give to see him smile at her one last time with his perfect teeth and green eyes, like a mirror-image to her own. To know he was finally at peace would mean the world to her.

"Alex . . ." Christian politely asked her to continue burning bodies with him.

She wiped away her tears and swallowed her feelings, refocusing on the task at hand.

25

Taking Charge

Blackheart flew over Meadowsville with his crows trailing him, looking down at everyone smiling and waving at him.

"They all trust me. They now pray to me. They need me," he spoke aloud to himself.

He was no longer needed for superficial reasons, like it used to be. Now they truly needed him as a savior. He smiled at their stupidity, thinking God would be so vain as to answer their insane request just like that. But let them be this way. If they hadn't learned after all these years, they deserved what was coming to them. First, he would build their faith in him as the beginning of his master plan.

He flew over the woods next to Meadowsville Elementary School and saw two of the former female construction workers feeding on a jogger under a dense patch of trees. Blackheart swooped down and admired them close up. They looked at him, dropping their victim, and they seemed afraid.

"So beautiful. But no longer needed," he proclaimed, waving the crows away from him into the trees.

The vampires leaped off the ground, looking at Blackheart with hunger in their eyes. They started to flank him, but Blackheart, with tremendous speed, flew over the vampire on his left. Before she could turn around, he effortlessly pulled off her head with one hand, her spine still attached, as he went back into the sky.

The second vampire fled but was caught by Blackheart in mere seconds. He still held her counterpart's head as he eviscerated the other vampire with a single claw. He took the heads of both women and left them on the front steps of town hall for the people and mayor to see his work. To further the narrative that he was fixing their unique problem.

* * *

When Mayor Wiggins returned to his office the following morning, he saw cameras taking multiple shots of the severed heads for the papers. He faked a smile for a few of the pictures, very scared of the end game. He didn't trust this monster at all, and if he could have controlled the situation and the council, he would have relied solely on Christian and Alexandra's input. He thought of their faces at the last town hall meeting, when he reprimanded both. He spit on the ground out of pure frustration with himself.

Several onlookers started cheering for Blackheart behind him. Blackheart stood tall atop of town hall, with crows lining the roof next to him, looking down at them as they celebrated his progress against Smith and his gang.

Blackheart locked eyes with Wiggins, giving him a look of superiority and smugness. The people now looked to *him* for protection rather than the local law enforcement or town administration. They now thanked *him* for the good things happening in this town and no one else.

Defeated, Wiggins trudged into his office, despising his decision to recommend Blackheart being resurrected. He wondered what would stop this omnipotent being from beginning to kill citizens again if it so chose. And there, of course, were no answers. Blackheart was an unstable force that could do whatever it wanted, and that was a terrifying thought.

Blackheart took to the skies again and flew over the town, hearing the various praises from the people. His people. His ascension to godlike status proceeded quicker than he had expected.

"This will always be my town," he said, feeling a strong sense of accomplishment.

26

Celebratory Broadcast

Rebecca watched the television as another news report on Channel 1 aired, wondering what time Adam would be home for his dinner, which was sitting cold on the table.

"Good evening. This is Chip Simmons from the Channel 1 newsroom. An awesome sight at town hall earlier today."

The camera showed the heads of the two female vampires on the steps of town hall and Mayor Wiggins smiling. Public Works employees were burning the heads and scrubbing out the blood using harsh chemicals. The scene cut to Blackheart flying overhead at tremendous speed.

"Well, I think it's safe to say Mayor Wiggins and the town council's decision to bring back our once feared and hostile local legend can be labeled as a positive thing. Any doubters need to look no further than the heads of two of John Smith's undead army, left for all to see. While many of us want to thank God, we can now look only to Blackheart. The man. The legend. Folks, if you don't believe in a higher power looking out for us, here is proof it exists."

The station showed several more shots of Blackheart flying through town, being thanked and praised by the residents.

"The word of these actions has spread to our neighboring towns, including Festiville, Veronia, Ofrenda, and Cardiff. These towns have recently come clean about combating their own supposed supernatural entities, each more distinctive and elusive than the next."

The camera cut to residents of each neighboring town asking Blackheart to come help them too. They offered gifts and shrines to him if he'd even just consider it. Several houses of worship were also shown with images of him being prayed to.

Chip Simmons was shown again. He performed a very fake and unenthusiastic laugh, smiling at the camera. "Sorry, folks . . . he's ours and we're keeping him. At least until he takes care of John Smith, then we'll see where he ends up. In other news, Lucerne Lake is still experiencing extraordinary levels of hydrogen sulfide. State and local health officers are now planning to build several types of aeration units to resolve the issue."

Rebecca looked at the clock, now realizing how late it actually was. Adam should have been home almost two hours earlier.

27

Resisting Temptation

Meanwhile, downstairs, Christian sat in his basement, looking at his armor. He had never cleaned it after it was peeled off his burned body last year. He just hung it like a keepsake—blood, sweat, skin, and all still a part of it. He planned to clean and polish it during his time recovering but felt that was too close to his old, unhealthy habits. It was fine as it was.

The suit began speaking to Christian, as it represented his past mindset.

"Remember how good this made you feel? How important you felt?"

"I do. I think about it a lot," Christian responded.

"No rules. No laws. Just results."

"Yeah," he said, remembering impaling Blackheart sixteen years ago. "I don't trust this. He can't be trusted."

"I wouldn't either. You know him so well. Would it be so terrible if you suited up one last time? To save the town once and for all? And your family?"

He admired one of the knives hanging off the utility belt. It was rusted but could still make a decent cut into flesh. The entire suit of armor had begun to show its age.

"I'd love it," he said, touching the reinforced padding around the knees.

"Try me on. It'd be between you and me. Just see how it feels."

"I can't," he said, thinking of his family.

"You coward."

"I'm not a coward," he replied indignantly.

"You think wearing a police uniform is going to do anything about that monster? You're not even a real cop. You're just a decorated civilian employee. They'll all be dead in no time. And then where will you be?"

"It's the right thing to do."

"Maybe not."

"But what if he is for real this time? What if Blackheart has changed and is a messenger of God?"

"I'd rather be safe than sorry. Wouldn't you?"

Christian looked at the burn marks up and down the boots and calves of the armor, thinking of when Blackheart set him on fire. He then saw the permanent scars from the thorns across his knuckles and forearms.

"How far are you willing to go?"

"As far as I need to."

"Imagine if you were like Blackheart. Along with this armor, you'd be an immortal force of reckoning. All your aches and pains would be gone. Nothing could hurt you ever again."

Christian imagined himself as a vampire. "I could save them all. We wouldn't ever need Blackheart again," he said, remembering his fallen officer.

He looked to the side and saw Caroline's old tricycle, which made him remember the pain and trauma that had almost broken him. He also recalled his Aunt Mildred and Uncle Marty, who told him his parents named him Christian for a specific reason. They were firm believers in God and named him hoping he would be their little Christian soldier who would uphold the beliefs they held so dear, no matter what.

He took a deep breath and came back to his senses. "But I'm not willing to do that to my family ever again. It was selfish when I did this before. And I swore before God that I would never let anything get in the way of my love for them again. Nothing. And that means you too," he fired out, condemning the suit.

The suit had no response. Christian stood up, feeling empowered by facing and defeating some of his personal demons once again, and put the tarp back over the armor.

"One man can't save the town. Everyone has to do their part. We just have to pray that God protects us from Blackheart and brings us all together. That's how this needs to end. Because without God, we're done for."

He began turning out the lights, and the suit spoke to him one last time.

"Are you scared?"

"Yes," he said, feeling genuine fear for the town's current circumstances.

He started upstairs and Rebecca came flying down the steps, falling into him.

He helped her stand up. "Hey, hey, calm down. What's wrong?"

"Adam was supposed to be home two hours ago," she said, panting.

Christian had been in the basement so long, he lost track of time. "Shit. Call him now."

Rebecca called Adam's cell, but they heard no response on the other end.

"Fuck, it went right to voice mail," she said throwing her phone in frustration.

"Okay . . . um . . . please don't panic. I'll go find him," Christian said, trying to keep his own emotions in check despite being in a full-blown panic.

"I'm coming too."

"No, please don't. He may come home. You need to be here in case he does."

Rebecca's lovely eyes became glossy, and Christian hugged her.

"Don't worry. I'll get him back to you safe and sound," he said, holding her.

She stood on the steps, tapping her foot, with one hand over her mouth, hoping her husband could keep his word.

Christian put on his shoes and rushed to his car. He called his former squad members and asked them to help find Adam.

Though neither said it out loud, both Christian and Rebecca feared Adam had become the latest victim of John Smith, especially after finding out about the attack at the library.

28

Final Plea

Alexandra watched the news broadcast with a heavy heart. She was petrified for the town and the fractured faith it currently suffered from. She and the small group of her fellow church leaders had continued their pursuit of their resistant colleagues, but there was still no progress. She had prayed every day since Blackheart had been brought back but received no guidance from God. She turned off the television and walked to the church. It was completely empty and dark inside, except for the stained glass windows letting in the last of the dusky sunset.

"What can I do?" She spoke to the large window in her church depicting Jesus Christ. "This town has been through so much. Why do we have to endure more?"

She thought of Blackheart's breath on her last year and how nauseated it made her.

"This is not the Second Coming. This creature is not a tool of God. I refuse to see it any other way."

She shut off the television and returned to her office. She sat down and began a new email message, copying all of the church leaders in Meadowsville. This would be her final plea to them for help before she took matters into her own hands.

Good afternoon,

I hope you're having a blessed day.

As you have all seen, we have witnessed some otherworldly occurrences in our town over the years, the most extreme of which is happening as I write this. The creature we refer to as Blackheart was recently resurrected, even after I personally laid him to rest last year.

We can debate whether God sent us this creature with good intentions to show us that no wicked soul is so far out of His reach that it cannot be rehabilitated and made into a powerful tool of mercy and positivity.

On the other hand, Blackheart may have been sent here by God to provide this troubled town with the ultimate test of faith. As we all sit here and worship him as a god, enjoying the theatricality as he brings us supposed salvation, no one is asking if he should be doing these things. Should we have asked God to save us? Or should we have all banded together and kept our faith and trusted in Him, and Him alone, fully appreciating that He knows best, above all others.

If you recall the book of revelation . . . the Apostle St. John wrote of a vision of the end of days. The rise of the evil one, the Great Tribulation, and the end of an age. As Satan was cast down from heaven, he brought about fierce beasts as he appeared as one of them in a dragon-like form, condemning believers in God and deceiving man. A great battle ensued with the angels and demons. People of earth retreated to caves and hid. The stars of heaven fell, the sun turned black, and the sky receded. But in the end, God prevailed and cast Satan into a lake of fire and declared the ultimate victory against evil. As frightening as it was, it demonstrated the full power of Jesus Christ and the dawn of a new era.

John Smith and his creations are these beasts, and Blackheart is the antithesis of Jesus Christ. I have no proof other than my logic and faith to guide me to this conclusion.

And we must prevent our town from falling into the hands of this being, before we risk more lives being lost. I challenge you all to look deep into your souls and make the right decision to come together and combat this imminent danger to Meadowsville. God entrusted us as his loyal servants to guide our members and the residents back to the one and only Lord Almighty. God is depending on us to put aside our differences for the greater good. So please join me on this journey to save our people and battle alongside God!

She sent the email and prayed again that her message would be received well.

29

Damning Discovery

Several miles away, Adam and Bruce hid in the woods by Chrysanthemum Drive and watched Smith with six of his vampires feeding on animals near the mansion. The boys were there observing the eating patterns of the creatures for their paper, which was nearing completion. After being attacked by John Smith and knowing how dangerous it was, they wanted to know everything about the vampires, even if it meant taking their research to a dangerous limit. Adam and Bruce didn't plan to be at the site this long but also didn't want to prematurely make noise and risk being found. Their parents would be worried, but they were stuck.

The vampires finished their victims and lined up, readying themselves for Smith to sample each one of their now fully engorged bodies. Just as Smith was about to nourish himself, they all stopped and looked up to the sky.

"This is so surreal," Bruce whispered.

"Just disgusting," Adam replied.

"Smith is so decrepit. Always imagined him being bigger."

"Well, he's been around for a long time."

"So this is probably what he did with those kids early on. He had them hunted and then fed on them like this."

A loud crash yielded Blackheart landing on one knee with a multitude of crows coming down alongside. None of the vampires moved at first, but they cowered in fear as Blackheart stood towering over them. His newer, very tall frame and grotesque appearance made Adam and Bruce flinch, but they attempted to stay hidden away.

He walked toward the group and smashed two of the vampires together, mashing their skulls. He pulled the next in half vertically and another horizontally. He used his left horn and impaled one, flicking his head slightly to launch the dead creature into the woods. This entire slaughter only lasted a few seconds but demonstrated the full power of Blackheart.

He turned to see John Smith, and anger rose in him that came second only to his rage at God. For the first time in a long while, the two powerful historical figures were face-to-face. This was Blackheart's abuser. The person who killed his parents and held him captive for years, sexually abusing him in various ways and making him watch the horrible things he did to the people of Meadowsville. But Blackheart comforted himself with the knowledge that he was no longer a victim or even a vampire. He was godlike and had nothing to fear from this person.

Smith, still much weaker and fragile due to his old age, smiled, sniffing the air. Several small plumes of dust exuded from the opening where his nose used to be.

"Timothy," he muttered. "Your smell is so fragrant."

Blackheart surprisingly grinned back at his enemy.

"Your blood flows strong, boy. I can hear it like a river. I imagine it being as sweet as your innocence. I'd like to have some."

He stepped forward, but Blackheart put an arm out, stopping him with ease.

"I'd love to send you back into the ground. But you're not done yet. I brought you back for a reason. You have plenty more damage to do to this place before I'll allow you to die."

Several ants crawled onto Blackheart's arm, and Smith quickly licked them off, making a handful of pleasing groans. Blackheart shoved him back several feet, knocking him over.

"You will not be spared," Blackheart said. "I'm running things now, you wretched creature."

"Your skin tastes as sweet as I remember. I recall how every inch of you tasted," Smith taunted, not caring about his own life. "I look forward to seeing you again, Timothy."

"I will be the one to end this town and the world. You can call me the Almighty. Just as the rest of these people will," Blackheart proclaimed.

He flew back into the night sky, holding all the dead vampire corpses in hand and leaving Smith unharmed.

Bruce and Adam were left speechless at the events they just witnessed. Would anybody believe them? Should they risk their safety by exposing Blackheart to the world?

Smith began to sniff the air, sensing the boys' presence.

"Here, little birdies," he whispered. "It'll be much easier if you come to me before I come to you."

The boys tried to sneak away, but Adam accidentally snapped a twig, giving away their location. Smith slowly walked toward them as both boys froze, unsure what to do.

"If we die here, no one will ever know what we saw," Bruce said.

"No one is dying tonight," Christian said, appearing out of nowhere.

He put his hands over both boys' mouths, stealthily pulling them into the woods and away from Smith. They reached Christian's car several minutes later, and he pushed them both into the side of the vehicle with force.

"Dad, I'm sorry. I—"

But before Adam could finish his sentence, Christian grabbed him and hugged him so hard that he knocked the wind out of his son.

"God dammit, I'm so glad to see you again. Your mom and I thought we lost you. I knew you two would come to this place. Are you stupid? Do you realize how dangerous this little stunt was?"

"Mr. Reed, we're doing research for our paper," Bruce added in, but Christian put a finger up to silence him.

"Boys. Get in the car. Bruce, you're going home. Your parents will hear about this," Christian ordered in a flurry of emotion.

"Dad, I have to tell you something really important."

"Not now. We'll talk about whatever it is later," he replied, too exasperated to think straight.

"But—"

"No. Later," Christian told him as he called Rebecca and the police to inform them he had found the boys.

30

Rising Above

The next night, Alexandra stood at the podium in her church. She had only a small number of attendees. Many people left after her decision to not support the resurrection of Blackheart. Others now saw worshipping him as a replacement for traditional churchgoing.

She began to speak, to start the service, when Blackheart walked into the church.

This was the first time she had seen him since his return. She shrank from his horrid appearance but remembered her father standing face-to-face with Blackheart and not being intimidated. His faith gave him all he needed, and she was no different. The two locked eyes as he moved toward the altar, and the congregation members lowered their heads out of respect for him.

He reached the altar, and Alexandra held onto her faith, thinking he still could not stand on the altar, just as before. However, in the next instant, he smiled warmly at her and stepped up, pushing her to the side.

"I never got the chance to thank you, Alexandra. You enabled me to reach the next phase of my existence. I always knew you were special. Much obliged," he said, winking at her with his enlarged lizard-like orange eyes, which produced a disgusting wet slapping sound.

She looked over at the holy water, and any other potential weapons, but realized things were very different now. None of that would affect him. Each time she encountered him, he took a different form and had altered powers. He had always been on a progression toward a higher level of being. And this was the height of that journey. And Blackheart's words to her confirmed he was as devious and manipulating now as he had ever been.

She casually stepped aside to avoid alarming anyone.

Blackheart turned to face the church members and address them. "Citizens of Meadowsville, I am not here to bring you fear. Nor false promises. You prayed to God for a savior, and I am here. I am the one and the only. The alpha and the omega. I ask only that which God Himself asks of you . . . to love and worship me. And when that is sufficient, I will be strong enough to put John Smith to rest once and for all. Meadowsville will be seen not only as a new holy land for all to come worship, but it will be at peace for the first time in its history. And beyond. Under my rule."

An optimistic tone filled the room.

"Now I ask that you follow me out of this house of God. Show John Smith you are not afraid. Because you believe in me. And I will protect you from him."

The naysayers began to support Blackheart and became livelier at his positive words.

Alexandra tried to interject but stopped herself. On her own, she was not enough to lead the righteous war on Blackheart. Until the other church leaders helped her, the town was at a very large disadvantage. The town was losing faith at a rapid pace, and she prayed once again that her email fostered a greater desire to work together on this guaranteed future conflict, that it reminded them of their faith and responsibility to God and their parishioners.

Blackheart led the people out of the church and turned to smile at Alexandra as the doors slammed behind him, letting in a whiff of rotten egg odor from Lucerne Lake. The stench was worsening, even with the aeration fans recently installed around the body of water.

Alexandra was left alone, full of determination and anger.

31

Breaking News

Adam and Bruce stood outside Mr. Edmonson's classroom, both very anxious.

"I don't know about this," Adam said. "Like, we have no idea what's going to happen. Might make things worse."

"I know, dude," Bruce replied. "I wanna piss my pants doing this, as much as you. But we've come this far. The weeks of research, the trip to the mansion, and all of it. We have to see it through now. Come way too far to just back out."

Adam and Bruce looked at each other, hoping for comfort. Adam was still not convinced of going in, so Bruce took the initiative to get him in the right mindset.

"You can do this. Promise. I got your back. We got this," Bruce said, patting Adam's shoulder stiffly, leading him in.

As they entered the room, Mr. Edmonson sat in the back corner of the classroom. He held his grading rubric on a clipboard, waving it like a small fan. While he questioned giving Bruce and Adam so much freedom with a topic, with the Reeds' history in the town, Adam would be the best student for this type of project. The class was involved in individual conversations between the paired students, and Edmonson broke it up to start the presentations.

"Okay, class. Quiet down. Our first presentation is Fuller and Reed, who will be attempting to explain the history of our town. I'm very eager to hear what they came up with."

Adam and Bruce stood in front of their modern world history class, ready to present the unofficial Meadowsville town history. Both were very nervous and understood what they were about to reveal was both informative and damaging to the town. There would be no going back once this information was released. And as their classmates heard it, they would take it to their parents, who would speak with their family and friends, and it'd reach the media within hours.

Bruce and Adam looked at one another, both with sweat on their brows.

"For our presentation," Bruce began, "we chose to attempt to piece together a basic timeline of Meadowsville's history. We did not shy away from controversial figures and feel that while this is not the final version, it is a much better and more accurate start than what is currently available to the public. We will also conclude with the connection that we feel links Blackheart and John Smith."

"One hundred twenty-six years ago, Meadowsville was a vacant oasis." Adam, now riding on Bruce's momentum, joined in. "There were no inhabitants here, while other nearby towns became colonized well before this point. There seemed to be a reason no one would come to this area and create a new town. According to the history books, there was an old belief that the land was cursed and would bring about nothing other than dark times. This was never fully explained until we heard of the founding families, the Smiths, Martins, Fitzpatricks, and Bensons. They were the ones who named the town."

Bruce took over again. "These families may or may not have been here at that point; however, we will assume they were, which is why no one else would attempt entry. As the books demonstrated, the surrounding towns, like Festiville and Veronia, had no dealings with these families, and they isolated Meadowsville. They all had baffling numbers of wild animals flocking to their towns, away from Meadowsville and whatever was scaring them off. As we took a deeper look into each of the other towns' histories prior to our founding families being acknowledged, there were many unexplained murders that took place by the borders of Meadowsville. There were reports of animals drained of their blood but the bodies left intact on the outskirts of Meadowsville— and even the occasional human. Was this a coincidence or possibly a direct link to the belief that there was some type of evil on our land? There was another large gap of several years, but one of the founding families remained, this being the Smiths. Unfortunately, Adam and I had the opportunity to actually meet with one of those original members of town the other day."

The class looked confused, as did Mr. Edmonson.

"Yes, we had the opportunity to speak with John Smith himself. He accosted us in the library as we worked on this paper and informed us that he killed the other families. With no books to guide us beyond that point, it was our assumption that all of these families suffered from a unique form of chronic porphyria. This is a group of blood disorders that yield some of the same traits as vampirism. For example, sensitivity to sunlight, psychological problems, physical deformities, and craving blood to replenish the blood not being properly processed in their bodies. Now, it's clear that what we've all witnessed by Blackheart is much more extreme than just a textbook medical condition. However, what he may be suffering from could possibly be an undiscovered or even covered-up specialized form of the illness," Adam continued.

"So it was our educated guess that with little to no food supply available, the founding families fought each other, with Smith being the sole survivor. There were no records as to what happened to his family, whether they died by his hand or during the territorial clashes. But there were stories out of Cardiff that Smith was spotted with a line of children following him. There is a strong chance that they were not of his family and were servants to him, being abused in the process, but they eventually disappeared too. So Smith lived alone for several years, slowly allowing outsiders to inhabit the area, and he kept a low profile, feasting on the scarce animals and the occasional settler he encountered," Bruce added.

"Over the next several decades, the town grew around him, and the reports of missing children rose. With no explanation available, early Meadowsville inhabitants grew tired of the abductions. They tried to hunt him but came up with nothing. The most that was captured were several photos of this mysterious man in black who would lead children away into the darkness."

Adam passed around the few real pictures of John Smith on record and continued. "It was not until much later on that we discovered John Smith was a known pedophile and mostly preyed on children. This continued on until present day, as the town grew and things became more developed. People came in droves, and the politicians began leading the town. Because of the massive rich land, the booming economy, and the money being made, Smith was pushed as a sideshow. Like something else people could celebrate by living or visiting here. It was the perfect plan. No one would think much about the occasional death or child gone missing. There were so many other good things going on. Much like consistent natural disasters, the residents and administrations kept things quiet, and made a large profit off of it."

"Now, at some point, Smith kidnapped a young boy named Timothy and had him prisoner for several decades until Smith passed away from natural causes. It's tough to say when this happened, and for how long, because there are no records of it. This boy, Timothy, grew up alongside his abuser, experiencing some of the most horrific circumstances imaginable. And when Smith died, Timothy took over the mantle, pretending to be Smith, when in actuality it was the entity we call Blackheart. We are making this conclusion based on the fact that there was no gap between Smith's death and Blackheart taking over for him. Timothy was the only one of Smith's victims who was never found dead. And because of Smith's known territorial mindset, if Blackheart was an outside party, one of them would have killed the other," Bruce said.

"Now, not much changed, and as the town continued to become developed and modernized, Blackheart basked in the spotlight, making himself an indispensable part of Meadowsville. Murder rates went up as tourism increased, and you'll notice that the crime statistics and homicide rates begin dipping with each mayor, going to their lowest with our former Mayor Valerie Wilkins. So we may never know how many people were actually killed during the development of this town and Blackheart's rise to power. Things were covered up, blamed on tourists, gangs, and whatever else, but were mostly kept under wraps."

"Sixteen years ago, Blackheart was killed by my father, Christian Reed. One year ago, he resurrected himself, demonstrating increased abilities, but was beaten by local church leader Alexandra Hughes. And more recently, he has done so again, praising himself as a god sent here to stop John Smith, who was also brought back."

"We took a field trip up to Chrysanthemum Drive the other night and were able to witness our supposed savior killing the remainder of John Smith's vampires."

The students started to clap and celebrate that fact.

Adam got nervous, and Bruce patted him on the back as reassurance that what they were about to do was right.

"But . . . um . . . Blackheart didn't harm Smith. We overheard him reveal that he brought Smith back on purpose. To terrorize Meadowsville and allow Blackheart to look like a hero. So that we would all worship him over God."

All of the students gasped and started texting everyone they knew in town with this story. Mr. Edmonson got up and stopped the presentation. He pulled both Bruce and Adam out of the classroom and into the hallway as his other students erupted.

"Are you two crazy?" Edmonson asked. "What are you trying to do here?"

"I think we said it pretty clearly," Adam responded.

"This whole thing is on a biblical level. And this town fed right into it. Just the way it is, my man," Bruce added in.

Mr. Edmonson told them both to go to the principal's office, just to get them to a safe place for now as he attempted to bring control back into his classroom. As he did, he heard each of the other classrooms all spiral out of control as the word of the conspiracy traveled quickly. Several parents of the students worked at Channel 1 and communicated the news directly to the station manager, who allowed it to be put on live TV that same afternoon. Within three hours, all of Meadowsville, and beyond, knew what was actually happening.

32

Smith Falls

Blackheart watched over the town from high in the skies. The crows he now adorned himself with flowed like a dark wave as he whistled to them. They covered him like a large black cloud.

He heard a commotion from the residents. It wasn't the praise he expected but rather displeasure. He then heard all their televisions say in unison, "Smith is a tool of Blackheart. Do not let him fool you. Repent now!" The sun shone brightly onto him as he roared into the sky, shaking every window in town, silencing Meadowsville. His plan had been discovered and was now in jeopardy.

His eyes began to sizzle with rage as he heard Smith below him, playing a violin, almost taunting him with old pastimes. The same instrument Blackheart was made to play by force, growing up as a victim of Smith. The violin he became proficient at and used to calm David as a young boy. Until his battle with Christian and David, that was the only piece of memorabilia that he had of his former predator. And now it would be the final interaction he and John Smith would ever have.

Blackheart was now sorry he brought Smith back but was eager to feel him die by his own hands. He thought back to destroying Smith's original violin, anticipating never hearing him playing again. But now here it was. A clear sign Smith had outlived his use. The only way to quickly restore the town's faith in Blackheart was to destroy Smith.

Blackheart quickly dove down toward the ground. The crows, unable to keep pace with him, flanked him from behind. Blackheart shook the earth as he landed, sending debris everywhere. Smith smiled as he continued to play the violin in the open patch of woods. He and Blackheart stared at each other. Smith motioned to the ground, and another violin sat in front of Blackheart. It resembled the one Smith left him when he died the first time. Smith wanted to play with his former victim. To see if his student had improved over the years.

Blackheart, in his own vanity, was unable to resist the temptation of the challenge and picked it up. Smith began playing a soft serenade piece, one that he had done with young Timothy many times. Blackheart remembered it well, as it was the very first and last song Smith had played for him. They began playing back and forth, dueling one another intensively. They eventually began playing in unison, perfectly matching one another, and finished the piece together simultaneously. The crows surrounded the scene, squawking uncontrollably.

Blackheart smiled at his victory of matching Smith and then crushed the violin with one hand, dropping the pieces all around his feet. Smith knew he was about to die. He put his violin down gently and stood up, watching Blackheart, motionless and silent. He was ready to die for good this time.

Blackheart exposed his forearm and reopened the scar he cut when he first met David as a little kid. He took the dripping blood on his fingers and flicked it onto Smith.

"Taste my blood. It'll be the last time that happens."

Smith dropped to the ground like a ravenous animal and licked the blood off the dirt, looking up to Blackheart with a gratified face. The crows all became silent and stayed in place.

Blackheart kicked Smith so hard that he was knocked past the treetops and into the sky. Blackheart flew up to catch Smith by one leg, now flying with him, slamming into the trees below, knocking them down. He then tossed Smith higher into the air and carried him by the neck over the town. Smith was heavily damaged at this point, and all he could do was try and sample more of Blackheart's blood as it dripped off his arm. As they flew over Meadowsville Community Church, a single drop fell onto David's still exposed body. Alexandra had not been able to burn his remains, which now found new life. The droplet was absorbed into the lifeless body, engaging the deeply hidden life force that all dead vampires in this state retained.

Blackheart threw Smith through a block of houses, demolishing each one, injuring and killing multiple families. Smith was now near death, but Blackheart feigned a difficult battle with him for appearances only. He needed to regain the town's faith in him and to put to rest any more propaganda that might harm his grand plan to wage war on heaven.

Blackheart carried Smith, destroying much of the town, using the body as a glorified battering ram. He wanted them to feel fear and uncertainty as he accomplished his mission of tricking them, all while getting his revenge on the villainous John Smith.

Very few structures were left standing, and there were tens of thousands of dead residents scattered. Meadowsville was destroyed. Blackheart made it a point to destroy all houses of worship, including Alexandra's church. His initial goal to make Meadowsville pay for its sins against him was now complete, and now he would demand dedication and faith from its surviving residents.

Blackheart flew to the town center and landed at the steps of the town hall. Several news vans rushed to the scene, cutting off ambulances and other first responders. The anchors and cameramen jumped out of their vehicles and filmed Blackheart. He held the lifeless and absolutely mangled body of Smith in the air with one hand. The power he now felt with his plan almost fully executed was exhilarating.

"This should answer any more doubts about my purpose here," he bellowed. "Why would your god allow this despicable being to be brought back? Why would He allow your town to be destroyed so many times? Why would He let so many of your friends and family die today? Where is God for you in all this? Let me tell you . . . He is a braggadocian sloth. He waits until things fix themselves and then wants credit. And He holds your soul hostage unless you dedicate your lives to Him. He is a worthless, overhyped deity. He apparently knows what you need better than you do. But me? I am here for you. I bring results like this. I will guide and protect you from Him now. I will do things my way. Which will now be the only way. Forget about what you know about faith and just hear my words. Worship me and me alone, and you will be greatly rewarded. And if you are not with me in my quest to dethrone God, you will end up just like this." He dropped what remained of Smith in a pile of mush on the ground.

Smith was dead. All the bugs he housed crawled out of his body, and the crows finally arrived, eating them one by one. The last remaining citizens gathered and bowed down to Blackheart. Most did it out of fear, while others genuinely believed in his agenda. With his demonstrated supernatural powers, the town being leveled, the religious leaders being divided, and no more religious institutions standing, Blackheart had now used everything to his advantage and had overtaken faith in Meadowsville.

33

Tough Lesson

Christian and Rebecca were outside their partially demolished home, which was one of the few that wasn't totally leveled by Blackheart's annihilation of John Smith. Both were helping injured neighbors get out of their collapsed houses, and they brought medical supplies and water from their basement to help.

Christian battled through his chronic pain, fighting off tears at the utter obliteration of their town. The town he fought so hard to save. As he jogged back into his basement for another case of water, he saw Adam wearing his armor.

Christian felt sick to his stomach, seeing his son making the same mistakes he made himself. He grounded himself and attempted to turn this into a teachable moment. "So you really want to do this?" he asked Adam.

"Yeah, I do. I have to," Adam responded, hurrying to secure the pieces of armor.

"Why?"

"Because I made this happen. This would've never happened if Bruce and I didn't give that report," he said in a frenzy.

"This isn't your fault. This was going to happen no matter what. You should be proud of that paper. You pieced it all together and brought everyone the truth. The truth is never wrong."

"I have to do something."

"Then stay here and help us. Look at this place." Christian pointed toward their neighborhood with the screams and cries of people in need.

"I'm so angry," Adam said, clenching his fists.

"I know how you feel. That fire inside of your gut. It overwhelms you. Takes you over and makes you do stupid things. Won't let you think straight," Christian said more intensely, remembering it all.

"You don't miss it?"

"No," Christian said after a brief, reflective pause, finally putting any last remnants of his old ways to rest for good.

"I'll tell you what I do miss. I miss all the time I didn't spend with you and your mom. Because of all this. I miss being able to move without feeling pain all over. And I miss your sister. I miss her every day."

Adam started to cry, thinking of the older sister he never knew.

"And I won't let you repeat my mistakes. I won't let this creature take you away from me. I will not lose another child. I love you too damn much," he said, embracing Adam, comforting him.

Rebecca heard the last part of their conversation and looked on, feeling elated with love for her husband and son.

"Now get out of that suit and help us. We need you here now. They need you. Just like I told you before . . . sometimes it's better to use your brain and not just your body. This is one of those times."

Adam listened to his father and grabbed a case of water, rushing it outside to an injured neighbor.

Rebecca and Christian watched him, proud of their son.

"We've done all right with him," Rebecca said.

"He's a great kid. We're really lucky," Christian retorted.

"I'm so proud of you both."

They kissed each other and were thankful for their family and blessings, even among the destruction around them.

34

Absolute Allegiance

Blackheart flew overhead, admiring the town being in shambles. The smell of death was in the air. He coasted above three residents trying to crawl out of a destroyed bank.

"Please help us," one shouted to him.

"Do you believe in me as your true savior?"

The woman hesitated, and he left them all to die.

He passed over Christian's property, looking down on at his longtime rival. "How unimpressive he now looks." Humanity had robbed him of his youth, power, and ferocity. Christian was no more of a threat to Blackheart than an ant.

Christian poured water on a child's face, washing the dust out of his eyes from the houses around them being totaled. He looked up at Blackheart, who stared down at him in victory, with his crows flying all around him. No more punches needed to be thrown. No more fires or battles. Christian's efforts had been squashed, and he knew it. But he also now knew that he gave it all he had. He remembered the feeling of helplessness when both his parents and Caroline were taken from him. He was left alone and troubled. Now he truly had to lean on his faith, keeping true to his fallen parents and their goal with what they named him.

Blackheart flew by his home on Chrysanthemum Drive to see a line of people leaving him gifts. Whatever they had left after his destruction was what they put at his feet. There was no more resistance. There was submission and loyalty to him. He smiled and looked beyond Meadowsville at Veronia, which had a solid police barricade to continue their practice of keeping Meadowsville's issues away from their town. The others had joined the movement and had no choice but to leave Meadowsville to itself and not interfere until the problems crossed the borders into their territory. Whether the problems were artificial or genuine, the neighboring communities wanted no part of it.

He passed over Alexandra's church as she was sifting through the debris. She looked up at him, and her gaze held nothing but rage. He sneered at her as his crows cackled, and he flew off. He had beaten them all. Meadowsville and all his former rivals were meaningless now. It was time to expand beyond this town and continue his crusade against God.

Alexandra kicked a piece of the roof that lay against her foot and yelled. She would battle Blackheart with every last ounce of her being. This terror would not stand. She pushed through the wreckage and found her vestments, soiled and dirty, but she put them on anyway. She then picked up the large cross that once resided on her altar. She had trained her whole life for this moment and had to go meet her destiny. The stained-glass face of Jesus was somehow still intact, and there was a single beam of sunlight highlighting it, casting a ray in the direction of Lucerne Lake.

"It's a sign," she said to herself.

35

Final Peace

Alexandra marched to Lucerne Lake, which was one of the only areas of town not affected by Blackheart's demolition. All the residents had left that area due to the health concerns, but it was now the safest place in town.

As she carried the large cross with all her might, she walked through the town yelling for everyone to join her. At first there were no replies, but slowly people started coming out of the debris and following her. She began crying at all of the injured people around her, some with missing pieces of their bodies, or carrying their children, who were either unconscious or dead. And then there were the thousands of slaughtered residents she passed who could not join. Pained screams and pleas for help filled other areas of town, but she marched on and led her followers. It was like walking through hell on earth, but she was not afraid. This was the end of things as they were, and the start of the way things would be. She was content knowing her involvement was so important.

She reached the lake as the sun set. All the aeration fans and barriers were knocked over during the destruction, and the smell was overpowering. Robert Levitan's corpse lay under the one fan, showing he risked and ultimately lost his life trying to do his part to protect the town. A few hundred people, the Reed family included, and a handful of her colleagues had joined in her caravan. She looked out at Lucerne Lake, which was calm, and slammed the cross into the moistened soil near the water. It stood tall and mighty, and she turned to face the people who placed their faith in her and not Blackheart.

"People of Meadowsville, we have reached the end of times. We have reached a crossroads where we must decide what our future is to look like. On one side, there is guaranteed salvation and peace. However, the other is a surefire trajectory to hell under the rule of a modern-day Antichrist whose only concern is to gain enough power and support to dethrone God. He has no apprehension about killing each and every one of you just for sport. And enough of us fell for his trickery to see him as the Second Coming. He is no such thing. Those of you who believed that were foolish, and we've been so for too long and too many times. This is why we keep finding ourselves in this same place repeatedly. Because we are too easily pulled away from God. This devil keeps returning because we give him our most valuable asset—our faith. And the more he gets, the stronger he becomes. And if we let this monster take it all from us, he will continue on after we're all gone, and the world will be in jeopardy."

Christian nodded at Alexandra, feeling as a proud father would seeing his child reach a major milestone. He pulled Adam and Rebecca close to him in the moment.

"But we can remedy all this by reaffirming our allegiance to our one true Lord. And He will provide us with the help we need. We should never look beyond Him for anything. He is always there for us, and while we may not understand His methodology, His priority is always our best interest. And anything who tries to make you think otherwise is a tool of the devil."

The crowd became emotional and comforted each other. More of her colleagues, most of whom were the individuals who refused to work with her to prevent this type of situation, were now standing by her side, finally working together with her. They walked to each person, asking them to hold hands and listen to Alexandra. A mildly injured Mayor Wiggins limped to the crowd and grabbed Christian's hand.

"I'm so sorry for everything, Christian. I hated it all so badly. I never wanted any of this to happen. I'm sorry I hurt you. And that I didn't act as the leader I should have been to these people."

"I know you are. Now grab my hand and let's put an end to this once and for all. The right way. The way you, Alexandra, and I always wanted to do it," Christian said, embracing him, remembering his valuable lesson in forgiveness with David sixteen years prior.

"We refuse to adhere to this monster's burdens any longer. We are better than this. We deserve better than this. Better than him. And God will give us the salvation we deserve. He will smite this devil as only He can. Lord, hear us all pray to you. Amen," Alexandra concluded.

The people closed their eyes and looked down, still holding hands in front of Alexandra. There was a new feeling of unity and faith in the group. They prayed individually and apologized to God, reaffirming their love for Him and asking for His blessing and support during this most serious of times. Their varied faiths and needs were communicated to God clearly for the first time in the history of Meadowsville.

* * *

Blackheart appeared overhead, staring down at the group, who felt his presence but refused to acknowledge it. They did the worst thing possible, which was to treat him as a nonentity. They took back their faith and put it in God, denying Blackheart's efforts, cutting off his power supply.

The crows flew away from Blackheart one by one, and he began to lose his abilities, resulting in him slowly floating to the ground, landing in front of the cross. He felt powerless, scared, and vulnerable—all things he hadn't felt since Smith took him from his parents as a child. He remembered what it was like to be human. He was now unable to hurt anyone, and he felt mortal for the first time in many years. He was no longer Blackheart and was now just Timothy.

Under a clear sky, an abnormally large bolt of lightning struck the lake behind them all, igniting it in an incredible fire that demonstrated God's power, shaking the world. The dramatic increases in hydrogen sulfide were setting the stage for God to show Meadowsville the true version of fire and brimstone. And he was calling for Blackheart to join Him once again, as his journey on earth had finally ended.

Blackheart looked at the fire and felt the wrath of God but then felt forgiveness. It warmed him deeply in his soul. He had not felt love like that since his mother hugged him as a young child so many years ago. Before all the unpleasantness that brought him to this point. Only God could give him what he needed now, and he understood that. All his losses and sacrifices over the course of his long, lonely, and perilous life were worth it to be with the Lord. His previous time in heaven was not accurate, and was God giving him more time to become humbled in order to fully appreciate the blessings of heaven and His companionship. All while making Meadowsville find their permanent salvation. God's grand plan was beautiful in its complexity.

Meadowsville had learned its final lesson and was completely destroyed, now able to purge the toxic residents and habits that plagued it for so long. And it could now rebuild as a more stable, faithful, and unified community. God had finally answered their prayers and any doubt as to his presence was silenced.

Blackheart looked at the residents, admiring the fire that made the cross light up. He began to tear up as he realized he would be entering the true kingdom of heaven—but now with a newfound respect for the process of death and the ultimate power God held, using it for good and never His own benefit. As Alexandra told him before, *"God never forgot about you. He saved you. You were more important to him than anyone else. And he'll always love you."* He had not tricked her a year ago, as he once thought. She had been right about it all along.

Blackheart looked to the people in the crowd with total forgiveness for his sins and a humble heart. He felt someone close to him and turned to see David, who had been resurrected when a single drop of blood fell on him earlier.

Alexandra saw David, with total peace in his body and soul, alive for the first time in almost two decades. Her tears began as they locked matching green eyes once again and for the very last time. Feeling the love for him all over again, she was being given the privilege of seeing him at peace, absent of all his human problems, and that was all she needed. It meant everything to her just to know he was okay now. David looked at Alexandra and smiled warmly, giving her total closure. And she now understood the message from God that she was ready to move on from Meadowsville. There were no more lessons to be learned here.

David was the only victim whom Blackheart truly regretted hurting. He saw a lot of himself in that boy and had hoped to give him all the opportunities he felt deprived of. But things, unfortunately, didn't work out the way Blackheart had intended. However, seeing his former protégé again warmed his heart, and he knew David was sent directly by God to welcome Blackheart back to heaven and to eternal peace.

David was not only able to see Alexandra one last time but was allowed to complete his original goal of taking Blackheart away from the town for good. David looked to Timothy and calmly offered his hand. Timothy took hold of it, and they walked together into the fiery lake, bringing about the end of all supernatural happenings in Meadowsville forever.

The entire town stayed holding hands and praying as a group for several more hours, waiting for the fire to extinguish itself. They all promised God to never turn their backs on Him ever again. Meadowsville had finally found its salvation.

36

Forever Changed

Several weeks later, Cardiff, Festiville, Veronia, and Ofrenda all had removed their blockades and opened themselves up to helping repair Meadowsville. There were mass memorials and ceremonies honoring the tens of thousands of people who died in town. The surrounding cities all now realized there had been no publicity stunts or alternate realities regarding what happened in Meadowsville. Mayor Wiggins worked tirelessly over his next several successful terms as mayor to rebuild the relationships with their neighbors, who offered their money, supplies, and residents to help rebuild Meadowsville into an all-new town. After several years, the construction projects were almost done; most notably, the house on Chrysanthemum Drive would be maintained, paying homage to the town's now accurate history, including a beautiful memorial wall for all lives lost, which Adam and Bruce helped develop. They were both honored as heroes after their research and fearless presentation of the first accurate depiction of the town's history. Adam grew up, staying close with Bruce, to serve in almost every major public office in town. He always listened to his parents' wise words, which kept him as a strong, stable, and incorruptible leader.

Lucerne Lake became a designated tourist trap, with a beautiful walking path around it, along with eyewitness accounts and artist renditions of *the lightning bolt that shook the world* presented for all visitors to see and believe in. The lake never had any further issues with pollutant buildup and was a safe destination.

Christian and Rebecca rebuilt the top level of their home that was destroyed, salvaging pictures of Caroline but not rebuilding the house as it had been. It was restructured to be slightly smaller and more appropriate for just three people and not four anymore. They would always love their lost daughter and cherish her memory, but her bedroom being maintained was no longer a necessity. They remained happily married and lived out their days in the town they sacrificed so much for. They spent their time volunteering and were paid hefty pensions for their efforts to save Meadowsville over the years.

That particular bill had been signed into order by Mayor Wiggins. He was able to structure the town's economy to be long-lasting and stable for the purest of reasons now. He and his wife, Eleanor, adopted several of the children whose parents were killed during Blackheart's attack on Meadowsville. They were able to have a family after all.

Alexandra saw to it that Meadowsville Community Church was rebuilt, but she left town shortly after. She kept in touch with the Reeds and found a position in a small church several hours away. She could truly apply her learned skills and help simpler people in equally important ways, as she did with her former congregation. She eventually met her husband, whose name happened to be Timothy, which she attributed to God reminding her of her hard work in Meadowsville and perseverance against Blackheart. Her life in Meadowsville forever changed her. Alexandra and her husband enjoyed a simple yet satisfying life together with their two children, Abby and Henry.

Once Meadowsville had been rebuilt, it was seen as a modern-day holy land, and people traveled to it peacefully from all over the world. They used it to help themselves reaffirm or further strengthen their faith. The residents in town who were still alive and able were happy to talk to the visitors about their experiences and personal journeys back to God. This helped bring a stronger sense of faith to each person, who would take home and let the good word spread across the world. Meadowsville was now free of any other preternatural occurrences.

THE END

If you enjoyed

RECKONING

be sure to read BOOK 1 and 2 of the Trilogy

This fast-paced adventure is a must-read for horror aficionados and lovers of all things that are scary, gruesome, and thought-provoking.

Welcome to Meadowsville!

CPSIA information can be obtained
at www.ICGtesting.com
Printed in the USA
BVHW062040110222
628753BV00001B/22